THE SOJOURN

THE SOJOURN

ANDREW KRIVAK

BELLEVUE LITERARY PRESS
NEW YORK

First published in the United States in 2011 by
Bellevue Literary Press, New York

FOR INFORMATION ADDRESS:
Bellevue Literary Press
NYU School of Medicine
550 First Avenue
OBV 640
New York, NY 10016

Bellevue Literary Press would like to thank all its generous
donors, individuals and foundations, for their support.
With a special thanks to the Lucius N. Littauer Foundation
and Jan T. Vilcek.

Library of Congress Cataloging-in-Publication Data

Book design and type formatting by Bernard Schleifer
Manufactured in the United States of America
FIRST EDITION
10 9 8 7 6 5 4 3 2 1
ISBN 978-1-934137-34-5 pb

For Irene

. . . That was how things were back then. Anything that grew took its time growing, and anything that perished took a long time to be forgotten. But everything that had once existed left its traces, and people lived on memories just as they now live on the ability to forget quickly and emphatically.

—JOSEPH ROTH, *The Radetzky March*

It's difficult with the weight of the rifle.
Leave it—under the oak.

—DAVID JONES, *In Parenthesis*

PUEBLO, COLORADO
JUNE 1899

She rises before sunup without waking her husband or the child still asleep in the Moses basket at their bedside and walks through the dark of the small shack into the kitchen. At the stove she rocks the fire grate, takes kindling and three quartered aspen from the wood-box, wraps them in newspaper and dried bark and heaps them on the near-spent embers, slides the vent for draft, then waits as smoke and threads of flame rouse and lick the underside of a worn and atramental gloss. From a pitcher she fills the kettle and places it over the heat, sits down, and stares absentmindedly in the dawning at an icon of Saint Michael the Archangel resting on a shelf cut into a corner of the wall, until she catches herself drifting, shakes off sleep, stands, and takes up another log to feed the blaze.

Her husband emerges from the bedroom and walks somnolent into the cramped water closet. She waits, listening through the walls (no more than partitions of pine crates cobbled together) as he hawks and spits and rinses the basin, then stands for a long while to relieve himself. He steps into the kitchen toweling his face, leans against the window, and peers blankly out at slag heaps and a smelter, all they can claim for a view.

Dobré ráno, *she says, not slipping out of the Slovak in which she dreams and thinks and speaks when she is tired.*

Hell of a racket, he says, and dabs behind his neck and the backs of his ears. You couldn't stay quiet for another half hour? Christ, a man can't even rest on the Sabbath. And I don't want to hear that damn language when it's just us.

But she is silent and doesn't move until the kettle begins to roil and she rises from the table, smooths her apron, and walks to a cupboard by the sink.

Coffee is ready soon, she says.

He hangs the towel on the back door of the closet and sits down in his own chair at the table, watches her slide a paper filter into a small steel funnel, place the funnel over what had once been used as a teapot, open a mason jar and dole out fresh grounds like a prospector handing flecks of gold over to the buyer's scale of weights and measures. She turns back to the stove, wraps a rag around the kettle's handle, and pours hot water through the apparatus. He bought the funnel in Leadville, where they lived before she became pregnant, and the coffee is black-market, beans siphoned off and sold or sometimes bartered by an old Hungarian man who had worked for years on the train from St. Louis bound for the hotels of Denver and San Francisco. She places the brew, black and steaming, in front of him, and he sips slowly and knows in spite of his mood that some manner of restiveness holds her.

I want to go out today and take the boy, she says, almost whispering but insistent. Just a short walk. Across the river.

His hands cup the drink before him as though it were a small world he might contemplate the fate of, and all of the enmity with which he rose dissipates with her request. The birth had been hard. The fetus was inverted but ill-positioned, and he nearly lost his wife from bleeding and *his firstborn from suffocation. But he had heard of the doc-tor who had been trained in Philadelphia (an easterner come west for anonymity) and lured him with payment in gold into the Pueblo shantytown on Good Friday, the last night of March 1899, and the man, stinking of ether, assisted the child with forceps and sutured the woman where she had torn. Eight days later, the priest came to the house, and the boy was christened Jozef.*

For the next three months, she was housebound, sleep-ing, taking what food she could, and suckling the child. She stood to do little more than shuffle across the sloping floor of the house, make toast, drink water, or go to the toilet. And these only when the child slept and she couldn't, for he seemed to bear his waking hours with a grief that was more than a newborn's discomfort with cold, hunger, and separation. When the boy cried, it sounded to her as though he was pleading with the body that bore him to remain.

The man nods. You two missed most of spring.

If spring is what they call it here, she thinks. The late snows and quick thaws, the mud that seems to grow and move as if it were some lower form of life itself, and the unbroken view of the industry that feeds them. The only beauty visible is as distant as the Spanish range to the south-west, which she found when they first arrived could be seen from the raised elevation of the railroad trestle over the Arkansas, but which she hasn't been able to walk across for almost a year.

It is morning now and she looks beyond her husband to the sky filling the top of the window behind him. A clear and cloudless blue matte, like it has never been since the coldest morning of midwinter, when she held the taut swell of her belly and wondered in her waking what kind of child it was that was being prepared for her.

The sleep was good, she says. I feel well. And she feels, too, the tension between them, born of where they are and where they wish to be, easing.

We have the meal with my sister and her family after the liturgy, he says. Go when the others are washing up. They'll understand.

You'll come with me?

No, he says, his eyes avoiding her to search his coffee again. I have to go up to Leadville tomorrow morning for a few days and I need to look over some maps. Clean my rifle. Mr. Orten wants to talk about the camp. Maybe do a little hunting.

What about work?

They'll have to do without me. It's slow, he says, and lingering between them is the memory of his nearly having lost this job for a similar absence just after she gave birth, the smelter boss having decided not to fire the new father. But he looks up at her and says in a tone that means he will say this much and no more, I think it's time we turned the land that camp's on for a profit, while there's profit to be turning. We could move away from here, Lizzie. California. Montana. We could move away.

She stands and moves to the other side of the table, holds her husband's shoulders from behind as though a boy himself too grown to cradle, kisses him on the top of his head, and in the other room the child wakes and begins to cry. She waits as the shallow bleats become sobs, then wails.

Go to him, the man says. And so she goes to him.

When he drank and someone was there to listen, he'd say that the Slavs of Pueblo had only exchanged life in one poor village for another, even if the journey to America, and then out west, promised to reveal a paradise. They had come for that purpose, and in the end it assuaged what hardship they found with the two things they knew well this side of the kingdom of heaven: work and family, lone virtues that reminded them of what was good about the old country. They clung to both so fiercely that a shirked responsibility was akin to what scripture called the sin against the Holy Spirit, and this fear bound them, because faith reigned like the quiet yet exacting old Rusyn priest, who had long ago come out to Colorado from Pennsylvania after his wife and five children died in a fire. Invisible to all but the old women throughout the week, he presided over the divine liturgy every Sunday and then remained with his small, obedient flock to share the midday meal at some parishioner's house, always sitting at the head of the table like a bearded and widowed grandfather to the disparate, self-exiled clan, and no one knew for sure that he wasn't.

Ondrej Vinich could just as well have lived out his days prospecting for gold and silver in the Sawatch, but this was the dream of a bachelor and the life of men in Leadville who were intimate with prostitutes and the ground. He had a wife and a child now, and they needed to eat, so his brother-in-law, a too-cautious man suspicious of any and all dealings that came out of Leadville, secured for him a position in the smelter and a vacated flat above a tack shop. Weighing what precious metal of ambition he had left against the rising sands of disappointment, Ondrej Vinich and his wife packed a trunk and came down out of the mountains, and John Hudak never let them forget who had delivered them from what he called a filthy town of gambling Protestants.

This Sunday she feels strong throughout the morning

and the service, until after the meal of dumplings and a chicken boiled in carrots and parsnips, when the now-familiar wave of fatigue overtakes her. So, she is given a reprieve from the dishes at her sister-in-law's and sent to lie down in a small room built like a porch off the back of the flat.

But she doesn't sleep, only lies listening to the women banter in their slangy Šariš and the dull clack of ceramic china as they dry and stack plates. Occasionally, like a breeze rising and falling at unexpected intervals through an open window, the laughter of children playing rises from the street, along with the metronomic clop of a horse on which rides some stranger inattentive to the Sabbath. Who could afford a horse on this side of town? she wonders. Or even want to ride it here for leisure on a Sunday?

Sunday is the only day the air isn't ashy and sulfurous, and on this day the weather remains pristine, even in the afternoon, when cloud cover often crests the mountains and sweeps down toward the plains. She stands, moves the child carefully as he dozes from his basket to a sling she wears across her chest, and steps out into the kitchen to say that she is going for a walk.

Tobias, the youngest Hudak boy, hears this as an invitation for the family in its entirety to go out, and he tugs at his mother's dress.

Matka, pod'me!

But his mother tells him that they can't go because there is work still to do, and it is Auntie Liz who wants to go with baby Jozef so that the two can get some air.

If he's underfoot, she says to Anna, I don't mind taking him with me.

Oh, Lizzie, he's always underfoot, Anna says, wiping her hands on her apron. She is pregnant, too, now, and near term, and bears her condition heavily not just at the hips but in her face and eyes with a visible disquiet. Go by yourself before it gets too late.

Tobias insists. Prosím, Matka. Pod'me, he pleads.

Anna wonders why the pull is so strong. If she hasn't paid him enough attention in the last several months? Or if it's her sister-in-law to whom her son is attracted, which is likely, she thinks as she considers the young woman before her as though for the first time, a face that shows no lines yet of age, a voice that speaks in notes of affection, which grace her infant son continuously and without conscious effort, and the angelic quality of possessing strength beneath a slight beauty, so that she seems to become a different woman altogether whenever she so much as turns her head or changes position.

At the table, the men talk and drink as though in another room, and Ondrej Vinich, who is indifferent to their company, rises and excuses himself. He hears the conversation between his wife and sister, sees them through the open curtain, and for a moment wonders who the beautiful woman with the sleeping child is. The distance between them pains him, and he regrets his harsh tone that morning and other mornings, so that he feels for an instant the desire to forgo his trip to Leadville and to walk with his wife for the few hours of quiet she seeks, but the thought dissipates. He says good day to the men and leaves the women and children to themselves.

Anna kneels down and says to her son, Toby, stay here with Mama and we'll have a treat of poppyseed and milk. You and me.

But Tobias begins to cry, and Lizzie, who understands why a woman should be so protective of her son, says, Let him come.

So her sister-in-law consents and Tobias dances a clumsy reel while his mother steadies him for his hat, points him in the direction of the door out of which his aunt has just walked, and stares after him as he bounds down the wooden steps.

Don't be long, she says to Lizzie, who is waiting in the street. I worry about him, you know. That boy has thumbs on his feet. And Lizzie promises that she'll keep him within arm's reach.

The streets and alleys of this shantytown neighborhood she knows well and has walked them for church, visits, meals, but as she moves past the farthest house she has been to in over a year, sees the smelter dumps huffing even while idle on a Sunday, and presses on in the direction of the river beyond a block of warehouses, she feels awake to the landscape so close and new to her, even in its filth and disarray. It could be close to Hell itself (as some have said) and she would still feel as though she'd been released into a garden. She looks down into the wrap that's carrying her son, and he's awake now, lips pursed and silent, his eyes azure beads gazing upward, a body content with her constant rhythmic movement.

L'úbim t'a, she says, and hugs him closer.

They come to the tracks before the bridge and Tobias hopscotches along the ties, but she knows—or thinks—there is only one train due on a Sunday afternoon and that won't be for a while, so she leaves him to his game, which he plays without any grace, says that his mother was right, and laughs when he teeters off a rail and tumbles onto the ground.

Som v poriadku, he says, smiling and dusting himself off. Then they come to the trestle at the river's edge.

For the first few minutes, they are both hypnotized by

the water. He is thrilled at the height, the roar of the strong course below, the distance he has been allowed to venture from home. She is drawn to the rise of the bridge from the river, too, and lets herself hang between the two emotions of daring and fear, then feels against her face the cool, moving air rising from the surface of the muddied water that has come this far south and east out of the mountains. Tobias points to a group of boys swimming in a back pool on the banks below, where the water's slowed and deep, and she clasps her forehead and mock gasps in a mime of disbelief that they should brave the cold. He pretends to shiver and can't control himself for laughing, until she moves out farther onto the bridge and motions for him to follow, and they make their way in the stop and start of looking down and moving along, as though explorers more enraptured than careful, until they find themselves in the middle of the trestle and Lizzie signals to her nephew that it's time they went back.

Before the eastbound passenger train number two approaches the river trestle near the smelter dumps in Pueblo, it has to negotiate a bend, so that when the engineer is in full sight of the bridge, the fireman is still in the blind of the curve as he stokes the engine for the run. To anyone standing on the bridge, the train is almost invisible until it has come around that turn and opened up to its full thirty miles an hour.

Lizzie sees the train as the engine makes the bridge, wonders how it could be. How could it be early? How could it be so quiet? Nearly silent, as though a moving picture.

But she sees then the whistle steam and hears its high note break through the sound of rushing water. And beyond the gray coal smoke the train spews, the sharp stretch of track that disappears back into the bending river, and (her eyes lifting) the farther horizon that the Sangre de Cristos frame majestically, she notices that the sun hasn't far to go before it begins setting. She wonders again to herself, *How can it be time?* She is more bewildered than frantic, and yet she knows, too, that she has moved slowly all day, as she has done every day since winter and so has learned to misjudge time.

There is as much distance before her on the tracks as behind. Maybe thirty yards. Not impossible ground to cover on foot, but here there is no place to retreat from the train's path, and the track on which she stands is all rail and ties.

We have to run, she says, and grabs Tobias by the arm. *Toby, come quickly,* she says again, and Tobias looks up from the water below, his face bemused, and she shouts at him now, *Toby, run!*

Tobias tries to run, but in as little as two steps, his foot is caught. He whimpers and pulls on it and begins to bawl as he tugs and tugs at the hobnailed boot that won't come free. *I can make it across,* she thinks to herself. *I can make it,* but that boy—he seems three miles, not three feet, from her—*that boy has thumbs on his feet,* she hears her sister-in-law say, and she turns back to wrench him loose, the sound of the train and its iron face growing, rising, she thinks, and she wonders if the entire cast of locomotive and cars might soar up and over them, but the boy squirms as he screams and screams, his foot twisting tighter into its trap, and no matter how hard she yells at him to hold still and be quiet, she knows there is no time to hold and, *Oh dear God,* she says to herself, *why can't there be quiet?*

The baby moves at her breast then, and she looks down into the wrap and there are his eyes, staring up at her with their otherworldly hue, he unfazed by the danger growing and bearing down on them, until she knows that even if she abandoned her nephew and ran for the edge, she would be caught before she could cross to any kind of safety. She catches a glimpse on the bank below of the lads, skinny and shivering, who have climbed out of the water to watch the Missouri Pacific thunder above, and so she removes the child from around her in one graced motion, cinches up the bundle, presses her lips to his face, and whispers, L'úbim t'a, then lets him roll from her arms out over the trestle and into the water as the braking train screeches and strikes.

DARDAN, PENNSYLVANIA
THE LAST NIGHT OF MARCH 1972

A ND SO I WAS SAVED BY THE SIMPLE ACT OF A BOY WHO dived into that river, icy as hell and too strong for even a grown man to swim, stroked hard to reach a babe sinking under the weight of the wraps that bound him, and floated to the safety of the opposite shore almost a half mile downstream. The Pueblo *Star-Journal* called him a hero, the rescue a deed that rivaled the world's greatest, and headlined their front page TRAIN CARRIES DEATH TO PLEASURE PARTY. Two days later, the paper long blown away, discarded, or used to wrap parcels and cuts of beef, the town had forgotten all but the reminder that death was indiscriminate.

But not my father, who knew that fortune, too, was equally thoughtless. Before the train set off again, the conductors took up a collection from the passengers, who chipped in fifty dollars cash, though more out of guilt than pity. And the next day, while the news was being hawked from the streets, the railroad company was writing Ondrej Vinich a check for five hundred dollars, in addition to paying the hospital and funeral expenses, afraid, no doubt, that I would die of pneumonia or some such thing, and there would be another round of headlines on which the story would drift farther east and west.

What the papers didn't tell was that Anna went into labor when she heard the news about her son, and the baby, a girl, was stillborn, and the woman's grief at the loss of her children nearly killed her as well, until the same doctor who had delivered me took me to my aunt (who lay empty and worn in her bed), placed me in her arms, and she nursed me with her daughter's milk and cared for me as we both recovered, and then brought me into her home as though I were her son, except that she and her husband never spoke again to my father and always left the house when he came around to visit me on Sundays, while everyone else was in church and he could be alone.

The following spring, my father took me east to Pennsylvania, where he had relatives and friends in the mining town of Wilkes-Barre, and we lived with a young couple who had come from his home village of Pastvina, looking (as he and my mother had years ago) for the opportunity due anyone who was willing to work and pray and accept the blessings that would be, as a result, bestowed upon them.

But all he could find was work in the mines, and he came back to the row house on Charles Street every night exhausted and coughing, so that I'd wake up, and the woman of the house, young as she was, chided him for disturbing the baby and asked him why he didn't take a shower at the breaker like all the other men, and he said that he just wanted to come home. He washed in the sink and ate soup with bread and a bottle of beer while I got rocked back to sleep.

One Sunday, these same friends took the train out of the city to the town of Dardan. "And I was so struck by this place," my father said, "its small center on a tribu-

tary of the Susquehanna that they called Salamander
Creek, and the farms, large and not so large, that radiated
out toward mountains that were in no way comparable to
the Rockies, but commanding in their own right." At the
local feed mill, he began to ask about hunting, and a man
named Zlodej, who was kin to the couple we lived with,
asked my father where in the old country he was from
and my father told him.

"But," he said, "I'd been living with my family out in
Colorado."

"Colorado," Zlodej said. "Now that's country out
there."

He said he knew a Czech man named Orten in
Leadville who could shoot a tick off a dog's ass, and my
father said, "George. George Orten." Zlodej asked him if
he was Ondrej Vinich and my father said he was.

"Heard about your wife," Zlodej said, and told my
father that he should come back in the fall and he would
take him deer hunting on his land.

The last thing my father did before he left Colorado
was purchase an M1896 Krag Jørgensen rifle, just like the
one George Orten had in Leadville. He wrapped it and
crated it and it came with us to Wilkes-Barre, and, after
me, it was, I think, the only thing my father really cared
about, and he waited and waited for the day when he would
get to hunt with it, and fire it, and dress what he killed with
it, as he had done in the days when he hunted with Orten,
and which made him feel, he said, "as though I was the
maker of my own fate."

All that summer and into the fall, my father worked in
the mines and clung to his renewed hope that he might yet
make a home in America. He picked and blasted and shov-
eled and dreamed of buying a small house in Dardan,

where land was still cheap and he figured he could find a job at a lumberyard until something better came along. Or maybe that would do just fine. And one Saturday morning in November, looking like a trapper he once knew in Leadville (but for the fact that he had shaved earlier in the week), he rose and, rifle case in hand, got on the trolley that ran past Charles Street and down along River, boarded the light-gauge train that carried most everything from Wilkes-Barre into the farming towns west of the river, and jumped off at the feed mill at Dardan corner, where he met up with Mr. Zlodej and another man he had never seen before, a man of means who was visiting Zlodej and looking into buying the feed mill and the 550 acres of land Zlodej owned and wanted to sell.

"I could tell right away that he had likely never fired anything bigger than a twenty-two," my father said, "and yet he spoke of having shot a lion in East Africa and hunted bear in the Colorado Rockies, and I said, 'Bear?' and he said, 'Grizzly. Yep, grizzly.' And I told him that Colorado wasn't the best place to hunt for grizzly, and regardless, grizzly wasn't the kind of animal I'd want to go after for sport. 'Well,' he said, 'then you ain't a sport,'" and my father decided right there that this was a man one did well to stay away from.

The rain that had fallen the night before in the city was snow in Dardan, a wet six inches of ground cover, and the mountainside they approached that day was a steep and wintry landscape of pine interspersed with hardwoods and outcroppings of rock and small caves, which Zlodej said were once home to the Susquehannocks when they roamed those hills before the Europeans arrived.

The snow gave fresh evidence of deer moving that morning, and Zlodej suggested that he retreat along the base of the mountain around to the other side, where there was a stream and large swaths of wintergreen patches, and he would drive any deer that might be grazing there over the mountain to my father and their hunting companion.

"I would have happily gone on that trek if I had known the terrain," my father said, "but I was stuck with the man hunting with us, and I began to feel so uneasy about his presence that I almost told Zlodej that I thought it was time I made it back to Wilkes-Barre, even though it was barely morning."

When Zlodej disappeared, his gait so quick that the woods were silent in an instant, my father suggested that he and the man find a hide from which they could observe the widest arc of the summit.

The man said, "Ah, we won't be seein' no deer anytime soon. Now lemme lookit yer rifle."

My father said that if he wanted to see a rifle like this, he knew a gunsmith who could show him one, and sat quietly with it resting on his knee. But on that mountainside in Dardan, the man got irate and said, "Who d'ya think yer talkin' to, son?" and without warning lunged and grabbed the rifle from my father's hands and shoved him hard against a rock.

"You see," he said, holding the Krag up and inspecting it, "I ain't used to hearin' the word *no*. That's why I aim to own most of this town, and Zlodej's mountain with it."

"What could I do?" my father said. "He wasn't going to shoot me, at least I didn't think so, because he didn't seem to know the first thing about handling a rifle like that. He just said, 'She's a beaut,' propped the Winchester he came with against a tree, and began to trudge up the hill toward a rock cave, carrying the Krag like it belonged to him."

And when my father asked him where he was going, the man said that he was going to climb over the caves to the top of the hill. "Got to have the vantage of height if yer goin to kill anything," he said.

So my father watched him as he climbed, the grade getting steeper and steeper, the snow-dusted tree line turning into a surface of packed dirt and wet scree, the man holding the Krag by its bolt like a shopping bag in his right hand and grabbing on to roots and saplings with the left as he struggled to ascend, until his foot slipped from the poor hold he had chosen on the next step and he pitched forward and began to slide and spin sideways down the hill, letting go of the rifle, which picked up its own speed and outstripped him as it dropped straight and slammed into a rock not twenty yards from my father and went off, shooting the man through the heart. He was dead before he came to rest.

"No one loved him, but he had a lot of friends," my father said, "or maybe people who clung to him for his money. Anyway, it didn't look good, no matter how much Mr. Zlodej came to my defense. I don't think anyone thought I was foolish enough to have killed him, but he was American-born and Philadelphia-raised, a Morgan they said, and I was a Slav, good for work and nothing more, an immigrant whose luck was bad since having come over, and getting worse by the day. I had to make some decisions fast, and I needed someone to take care of you."

So he wrote letters to what family remained in Pastvina, a small Rusyn village in a far northeast corner of the Hungarian Empire, and through negotiations with the local priest he arranged to remarry. The woman, whose husband had been killed felling timber, needed someone to support her own two sons in return for care of a child. So, after what he said was a long, long winter and late spring, around about the time I turned two, we packed a trunk and boarded a ship in New York harbor and made our way back to the country from where he'd come.

As a young boy, all that I could claim of my mother was a face I had seen in a daguerreotype my father had brought with him from America and kept next to him wherever he slept. And because I always shared his bed, that framed and static vision of the woman, who appeared somehow meek and stern in the same stilted pose, entered my memory from early on, and it was on the crossing back to Europe that I had—I hesitate to call it a dream, I was so young, but the memory of her in my presence then is strong to this day—the first dream of her that I can remember. She didn't speak and she didn't move; she just stood before me, radiant and iconic, her arms outstretched without beckoning, as though having held something she had just let go. Only her face was changed. Instead of the motion-less and serious demeanor the photograph held, her fea-tures wavered and I felt anticipation that she would speak and move, and that if I woke, I would find her among us, as she had been once before, living and breathing and whispering to me.

But even as my father sought, for his own reasons, to give some life to that lifeless past on an early summer evening in June 1916, while dusk settled, too, upon the whole of the Austro-Hungarian Empire, it came too late for me to understand or even forgive him, spent and weakened and alone that he was in the light of the candle flame around which we sat in our village hut while he talked and drank plum brandy and told me of what he had done and wanted to do in those last few months of life in America, before he took me to the old country. Over the years of my youth and young manhood there, he had decreased while I struggled to increase, bent that I was on the promise of a journey to the edge of the culture and land in which I had been raised and believed was my own (although I was, in truth, a stranger), with the imagined valor of heroic battles, and the thought that death would be a thing I doled out to others who dared resist. For, by the time I had heard the story of my birth, and my father's leaving the land of my birth, war was imminent, and I was hungry to call myself Infanterist, Frontkämpfer, Soldat. Anything. Anything but the son of the shepherd, because shepherd was all that my father—once he returned to Pastvina—wanted to be, and I wanted to become what he was not.

IF, WHEN WE, A LOST-LOOKING FATHER AND HIS RETICENT SON, first arrived in Pastvina in 1901, the people of our village had heard or whispered among themselves tales of prospecting and silver and the dangers—gunfights and murders—of the Wild West, stories they should expect a man who had seen that world to weave with suspense and nostalgia in their presence, they were soon forgotten, for there seemed nothing about Ondrej Vinich's attitude or demeanor (against the fiery young man intent on leaving Pastvina to make his fortune) to suggest that he'd ever lived one of those storied lives, but in fact seemed content and almost grateful to have to take up what was the loneliest existence a man could live in that part of the old country. Which is strange, when I think about those villagers and how they seemed to cling to one another and yet blame one another for the harsh lot from which not one of them could escape.

"Someone who makes it to America," my stepmother used to rail, harridan that she was, "and you come back! With barely enough to keep a house and pasture other people's sheep, while I'm left here to do all the work and raise my sons?"

I hear her now, old Borka, for that voice embodied my own fears as a boy, fear of loneliness, abandonment, and starvation, fear I struggled at any cost to overcome.

Every family in Pastvina had a child who died before the age of two from disease or malnutrition, because there were other, stronger children who might survive. Houses had straw roofs and a single fire for warmth, so that inside it was either bitter cold or so choked with smoke that you'd rather freeze outside than suffocate in. There was meat when someone slaughtered livestock, snared a rabbit, or (as my father could) shot a deer. Vegetables in the summer, but only potatoes, coarse bread, and root plants in winter. Children who'd lost a father stayed close to their mothers, whose sole existence seemed to be the upkeep of whatever hut they were given to live in, if they weren't lucky enough to remarry. These were the kids who hacked like tuberculars, eyes sunken and knees bowed, and who were usually dead before they turned five, a path I might well have been on, for (my father said to me years later on a morning when I saved his life) when he came down from the mountains after his first summer, he feared that I was one of those in this world who simply would not thrive.

But when he returned early in the following year because of unseasonable snows, he saw how Borka fed her sons all they could manage (and then some), set her own good portion off to the side, and left barely enough for me to eat, twice a day at most. He knew then that he had chosen poorly in that marriage, and wondered for the first time (the fear that would grip him and lead to his decline) if losing me, finally, might be the unintended consequence of the grief and desire for seclusion that blinded him.

And I remember still that fateful moment in the direction my boyhood would turn from then on, the day my father cornered my stepmother in the kitchen and demanded an explanation for why she fed me so much less than her own sons.

She scoffed at him. "There isn't enough for even three to eat squarely. But whose fault is that, eh?"

My father—a man whose descendants must have been a direct line of the old Kievan Rus, for his face looked carved from rock maple, his hair the texture of bear's fur, and he stood a full foot taller than any stunted villager who walked next to or past him—rose up in front of his wife and thundered, "My work feeds us all, and my son will eat first, or I will leave you and your boys alone to starve."

She shrank from him but, even wounded, barked back, "What do you know? You're never here half the year. I will say who eats and who doesn't. Go back to your sheep and your bed in the mountains. Father Bogdan will hear about this."

"I've already given Father Bogdan too much money for this match," my father's voice boomed, and she ran from him in fear. "If my son dies," he said, "they'll welcome you and that thieving priest both in Hell."

"He'll hear of this!" she screamed, and locked herself in a tiny room off the kitchen. "He'll hear of this!" But her voice and her intentions sounded weak and muffled through the door.

"He won't have to," my father called back as he

swept me up and carried me out of the house. "I'm off to tell him myself."

From that day on, for the rest of the winter, my father and I ate together the same food at the same table, and if my stepmother so much as lingered or addressed either one of us with even passing comment, he would say in a hard, flat tone, "*Chod' preč*," and she would slink away like a dog.

In spring, he must have decided that I no longer needed the care of my stepmother. For on the first Saturday of Lent, after he had packed the mule and saddled his horse, he asked me if I wanted to go with him for a ride. When I nodded yes in amazement, he said, "You had better get your coat and boots, then, because we're going to ride for some time."

Strapped into the saddle of the piebald horse he had bought from a Gypsy ("The best purchase I'd ever made," he said the day we put that horse to rest in a meadow grave), I traveled with him and the sheep and Sawatch the dog out of the village and up into the mountains of the Carpathian range, where we lived for the spring and summer in a cabin he built himself, and returned for the production of bryndza, to sheer the sheep, and for winter, when he tended to the animals that were his and repaired tack for another season, a cycle that would come to define all that I knew and loved of life.

When Easter came early, it could be bitter cold in the mountains for the first month, but the cabin was built of stacked logs around a central hearth (he had seen this done in America), and the walls were sealed with a mortar he made from clay and straw. The roof was pitched and over-hung the walls outside, so that the weather took little toll on them, and the inside was finished with the same milled planks he had used on the roof and no drafts encroached, the fire burned steady, and he hung his pots, skins, and my mother's icon of Saint Michael the Archangel on the wall.

The sheep we tended were used to being outside year-round. I did what work I could as a child, busy work I no longer remember, but soon was put in charge of the feed bunks, which we needed until the first spring grasses shot through. My father crotched the ewes before they gave birth, and then played midwife to entire flocks once they started lambing in late April, often with the help of Rusyn peasants who knew just when to show up every year and who seemed fond of my tall, independent father. Come summer, we moved each day through valleys and meadows, where we slept outside if we had gone too far from the camp or if the weather stayed clear, and talked on those nights of neither the past nor the future, but simply of what we had found strange, onerous, or beautiful that day (his division of the things of nature), and where we might lead those flocks the next.

All this time, we spoke in English. The first day he hoisted me into that saddle and we led the herd away from Pastvina, the last he spoke of any Slavic language was to those same Rusyn peasants who greeted him as they took to the fields in Lent with "*Slava isusu Khristu,*" to which he responded "*Slava na viki,*" and then ceased to say a word comprehensible to me, until, by the end of the summer, I knew—and could respond to—the language that was to become our own there in the mountains, and which he insisted that I never speak when we went back to the village, where everyone spoke Slovak, or Rusyn, or Hungarian to outsiders.

My father had brought several books with him from America (including a Bible and a dictionary), books he

kept on a shelf in the cabin and, after the midday meal or
when the light hung on in summer, would read to me,
sometimes having me take a chapter when he wanted to
rest or smoke, so that in time English was the first language I could read well. Thoreau's *Walden*, a slim volume
of Walt Whitman's poetry, a large, tattered version of
Herman Melville's *Moby-Dick* (which we read from so
often, the pages fell out), and, my father's greatest treas-
ure, the personal memoirs of Ulysses S. Grant in two vol-
umes bound in leather and kept together by a length of
hide. And so, America became for me on those nights not
a place but a voice, the voice of one man sitting alone at
his table and telling another of what he had seen and had
made—or would like yet to make, if there would be
time—of the world.

IF I COULD HAVE CEASED WHAT PENDULUMS SWUNG, OR WHEELS
turned, or water clocks emptied, then, in order to keep
the Fates from marching in time, I would have, for
though it is what a boy naturally wishes when he fears
change will come upon what he loves and take it away, a
man remembers it, too, and in his heart wishes the same
when all around him he feels only loss, loss that has been
his companion for some time, and promises to remain at
his side.

It began one day in winter, after I turned nine years
old, when the magistrate came to the village, knocked on
our door, and ordered my father to send me to school in
the spring term.

I didn't understand what he meant when he told me
that I couldn't go with him into the mountains that year
and instead must ride on the back of a cart into Eperjes,

where I was shown to a room in a dormitory with two other boys, told to dress in the red-and-olive-green uniform that hung in the closet for me, and in the morning marched with the rest of the children into the cramped room of a schoolhouse off the main street and a few doors away from the Greek Catholic seminary. I felt betrayed and so unsettled that I would not sit at the desk assigned to me, even when threatened with corporal punishment, with which the headmaster obliged. And after a week of beatings so hard and of such duration that I wept, they beat me all the more, and stopped only after I could neither speak nor cry and came down with a fever so bad that I heard the headmaster say that he feared he had gone too far this time.

That night, in an infirmary I don't remember being taken to, I dreamed of my mother. She was the same wavering and lucent image that came to me first on the boat from America, and who stood before me, arms outstretched, every spring on the first night I spent in my father's mountain cabin. Now, in my bed of fever sweat and wet sheets, she stood at my side and wiped my cheeks and forehead (for I felt the cool comfort of a cloth), and then she kissed me and I slept. And in the morning, after a breakfast of boiled eggs and mint tea, I returned to my dormitory, and to the classroom the next day, where I was told to take my seat, and did so without incident.

The lessons were rote, the teachers shrewish, the schoolboys I sat among filthy and unruly. I felt like a trapped animal living inside of a cage in the city (and indeed the school itself was a sort of jail, damp and cold and surrounded by iron fence work), my body weakening, my senses becoming dull, and the intense fear and need for self-preservation I once felt seemed long ago (though I had been there only a month) to have turned into a resignation that this was somehow all I could expect of life.

As the days lengthened, though, and the weather turned fair, we went outside at noon if there was no rain, into a dirt courtyard, where the other boys kicked a ball or scrapped with their fists, and I stood off to the side, leaning against a stone wall and listening to the long midday ringing of the Turkish bell (which our village church also rang and which could be heard far into the mountains on clear and windless days) until I was noticed, or until someone decided that I had been watched long enough, and I was taunted for being blond and unblemished and solitary, and so dragged into a fight.

But I was as angry about being in this company as I was quiet and bantam, and responded so quickly to the threats from my insolent schoolmates that the aggressor—a big-boned kid whose skin was gray and smelled of stale sweat—was forced to defend himself when I singled him out as the one to go after and began, without the hint of emotion, to throw hard and punishing blows to his head and body. I had never seen anyone fight and I had never been taught to defend myself. But I knew hurt and never wondered that day what it was I had to do if I didn't want to be hurt again. I set my feet, took a breath, and swung my fists so as to go through anyone foolish enough to face me.

In the end, my coat was torn and my nose bloodied, but I otherwise held my ground, and when that boy dropped to the dirt, I stood over him with my foot on his chest until he begged me to stop, and I pushed down harder out of anger that I had been sent to this place, when all I wanted was to be with my father in his cabin, and the boy ceased bawling and began to thrash and gasp for air, and all of the others looking on went silent, until someone said out loud "*Stačilo!*" I stepped back, kicked him hard once more in the teeth and walked away.

After that, they sought out weakness elsewhere. I learned my sums, and I learned to read and write Hungarian, which is all we were expected to learn in school. And when the year was over, my father took me back into the mountains, the magistrate never returned to Pastvina for me, and my life, I thought, would resume as before, but for the pendulums, wheels, and water clocks.

BEFORE I HAD HEARD ABOUT COLORADO AND LEADVILLE, THE Sawatch Range, and a man named Orten, my father's skills as a hunter were qualities I took for granted in the mountains, like hearing to a musician or sight to a painter, and what he taught me of marksmanship became, in the end, my only grasp on life, until I, too, laid down my weapon and went home.

The first spring day I went with my father into the mountains, I remember being fixated on the sight of the Krag as he unwrapped it from its leather cover and hung it up on pegs on the wall by his bed. The finished wood stock, shiny bolt, and bluish black metal of the barrel stood out amid the rest of the worn and beautyless tools and equipment and clothing that were part of the daily life of the shepherd. I always wondered how he managed to ship it from America, get it past the corrupt and greedy customs agents, and keep it from the curiosity of my step-brothers before lashing it to the horse's saddle. And every spring when we arrived at the camp and he took the rifle down from the horse's side, he'd always say, "We treat this as though its life is more important than our own, because one day it just might be."

When I was ten (the year after I had left school), he taught me how to remove the bolt, clean the barrel, load and unload it, all without firing a shot. And then, a month after we had brought the sheep into the mountains, set them grazing, and waited for the lambs to start coming, he said, "It's time you learned to shoot."

I went mechanically, yet with a practiced ease, through my test of assembling the Krag, and we hiked up a promontory, where we wouldn't spook the flock, and I felt as though I had already gone through a rite of passage and that on the other side there waited for me my first portion of the kind of strength my father possessed, as though it were a gift he had carved and prepared for me, and I felt a consoling peace in that, and pride.

But I did poorly on that test, clinging loosely to the stock with my face down, in spite of my father's instruction to "pull it in close and snug," and he yelled "Stop!" before I could lose an eye or dislocate my shoulder, took the rifle away from me, and said, "It's to be feared, but not fired in fear," and I wanted to assure him that I wasn't afraid, but instead I remaincd silent, and so we returned to our books and shepherding for the rest of the summer.

In the fall, I got a second chance, sighted down a buck in a high-mountain meadow, and, in my excitement, snatched at the trigger. The recoil on the Krag was so powerful that the shot went high and wide and the buck turned to look at us, sniffed in the wind, and bounded off into the trees.

"I think you scared him," my father said, and what I had initially felt as pride emerged then as my first bitter taste of weakness and failure, and I wondered if he thought less of me, thought that I was undeserving of his gift, or believed that I could not do the work he had for so long trained me to do, and quietly I waited for him to suggest that I stay home in the village, or even to send me back to school, when it was time to lead the sheep again to their summer pastures.

But the following spring we set off as we had done the year before, and halfway up the mountain he told me that I wasn't to go any farther with him. I trembled and expected the worst. He sat his old horse there on the trail like Grant astride his beloved Cincinnati, removed the Krag from its skin, unloaded it, and handed it to me where I stood on the ground.

"You go ahead, but don't let on to where you are. I don't want to see or even hear you. I'll meet you at the cabin for supper."

I stood frozen and staring up at the man.

"Go on," he said. "I'm going to be a while with these beasts, but Sawatch and I will get by."

"What am I going to do with this?" I asked, and held out the Krag, cradled in my arms like a baby I was unaccustomed to holding.

"Nothing, I hope. And if you knock that sight out of line, you can be sure you'll never carry it again. Now get."

I reached the cabin in a few easy hours, placed the rifle on its pegs, swept the winter dust and droppings, and waited.

There was silence all about, none of the sheeps' constant bleating, and no hint yet of their mephitis, which saturated the air and our surroundings once the summer months settled in, but to which one simply grew accustomed, and I enjoyed the strange sameness and yet difference about the place.

After a few more hours alone and with no sign of my father, though, I became nervous and decided to go back and see how far he had yet to come. And when I reached a small cliff and could just see the trail where it emerged from the forest, I noticed him standing there eating an apple and watching me, the horse grazing, the dog running a few strays up out of the trees.

"I thought I wasn't going to see you until we got to the camp?" he called out.

"I . . ." I stammered. "I thought you might need some help."

He pitched the core into the brush and said, "Sure could. Come on." He whistled for the dog, and when I scrambled down the side of the cliff, he handed me the bridle strap of the horse. "Take the flock. Sawatch and I'll get the rest of the strays."

That night, after dinner, he asked me if I had understood what he was trying to do, giving me the rifle to carry on the trail. I said no, I hadn't, and he nodded his head as if to say, I thought not.

"I wanted to see if you were predictable."

I told him (the tone of disappointment in my voice unmistakable) that I would stand in front of a train for him.

"That's not what I said, Jozef. I'd never question your loyalty. I said you're predictable. I wanted to see if I was right about what you'd do, and I was. I knew that if I sent you on ahead, you'd move fast, and reach the cabin, and that you'd turn right around and come back to me. I was betting the distance of the forest trail and one apple. And there you were, just as I expected. Now, if you want to learn how to shoot, and how to be a good hunter, you've got to learn to predict, but, more importantly, in yourself, how to be unpredictable."

That summer, he sent me out to hide and watch him herd. I had to make notes of how he worked, where he

stood, details of the terrain around him, without him
finding me. It was a game we were to play, and we played
it month after month. If he saw me—a glint from a buckle,
a stone I'd kicked loose—he'd drive the sheep in my
direction, which meant I had to get up and move, and the
more I moved, the less I could observe of him. At dusk,
when we met back at the camp or built a fire and slept
out, we compared notes. I could fire the Krag only when
I had more information about him than he had about me.

It was August before I could scratch more than two
details to my father's five, and in that time I came to
understand what he meant. Which way was the wind
blowing? Where was the sun? What was my target? How
big or how far away? Was it moving or stationary?
Distracted or attentive? At work or rest? Could it see,
hear, or smell me? Could I have slipped away from where
I hid as easily as if I'd stayed, unknown, unnoticed, and
unafraid?

I learned how to move when he moved, remain when
he remained, anticipate a turn because I saw the lip of
rock before he and the flock did, or knew exactly which
gill they would follow because its course was the path of
least resistance. My father was loath to waste a shot, so
practice was always some form of a hunting party, which
meant that we ate well in the mountains, and that fall I
killed my first deer. I did everything right—found my
position upwind of him, watched him emerge from the
cover of wood into a wild and fragrant crab-apple grove,
and made sure my shot was clear. Prone behind a fallen
tree that served as a good barrel rest and gave me a slight
height advantage, I snuggled my cheek into the weld of
the stock, reckoned that he was little less than a hundred
yards away, filled the fore sight blade with the front of his

body, took a deep breath, let out half, held, aimed just behind the shoulder of the foreleg where the heart is, and pulled the trigger.

LATE IN THE AUTUMN OF THAT YEAR, A WOMAN CAME TO THE door of our house in Pastvina. She was dressed in a coat two sizes too big and wrapped in a shawl on top of that, and she was weeping, looking as though all that she'd ever had was lost but for these few articles of ill-fitting clothing. She knew my father's name, and he embraced her in return. A boy stood behind her, his stature and expression the exact opposite of this woman who led him. He was tall, gangly almost, the coat he wore too small and thin for the first snow and wind, although his face gave away nothing of whether he felt cold or comfort. I stared at him and he stared back, his eyes a deep beryl blue, his hair (when he removed his hat) as fine and blond as mine. It was as though I was looking at my older brother, who himself seemed nonplussed to have found me. After a long conversation with my father (her words indiscernible at times through the sobs), the woman left. The boy slept on the floor in the kitchen that night and the next, until my father built a bunk bed above me in my corner of the house and that's where he stayed for the rest of the winter.

His name was Marian Pes. His mother was a distant cousin, a woman for whom, when they were children, my father had a fondness because of her own restless desire to leave the village and see something of the world, and the two stole away from chores in the afternoon to climb the hills that framed Pastvina and lay down in the new-mown hay, where they planned their getaway together. Eperjes was the farthest she got, where she worked as a dishwasher in the kitchen of an old hotel. (My father married my mother and left for America not long after.) When she became pregnant by a man who promised to marry her and then disappeared, the bishop (who had seen her attend the divine liturgy every Sunday) gave her a housekeeping job in the priests' quarters at the seminary, and when her time came, she named the baby boy Marian out of gratitude and devotion, wondering, perhaps, if he might one day sweep down those same tiled hallways wearing the black cassock and an attitude of meditation.

In time, though, the local priests and their parishioners talked. The seminarians were disedified, they said, and so she left and drifted through what jobs she found to keep her son in food and clothing, until she wound up back at the hotel, this time serving coffee to the men who read their newspapers in the lobby each morning.

She caught the eye of an older gentleman from Budapest, who wished to have a mistress when he traveled to the Šariš region on business, and so she lived under his care (and happy, it was said, the man even treating the boy like a son) in a small but elegant flat in the center of town for many years, until he died at his home, surrounded by family, and she was forgotten. She didn't know where she would go or what she would do, she told my father the night she showed up at our door after months of slipping further and further into destitution. She only knew that the fates had turned against her, too, as if she'd been cursed somehow, and she wanted her Marian to escape the same, if he could, to live somewhere besides the streets and learn something more than how to steal food from hotel kitchens.

When she asked my father if he would do this final

kindness for her, if he would take her son, though she feared she couldn't bear it, my father said, "I will treat him as though he were my own." And after a lull, as she turned to go, he asked, "What will you do, Zuska?"

Lowering her eyes, she said, "God's will," and they must have wondered then, those two, how the children who had lain on a hillside and dreamed of life in far-off places conjured for escape like fortune-tellers could have known how much of that dream would come true.

In the first few months of his living with us, Marian remained aloof from all but my father. He spoke in a mannered Hungarian, which I suppose he had picked up from his mother's lover and the other men who gathered at the hotel when they weren't concerned with matters of business, as though it were the extension of some salon they frequented in Budapest. But to look at him, there was no mistaking him for the child of the streets that he had become.

He never spoke of his mother. He rarely spoke at all. I remember my father handing him a thin yellow envelope every other week or so, which Marian would push into his coat pocket and then disappear. When he returned, he looked more aloof and sullen than before. And then the fights would begin.

My stepbrothers, Tibor and Miro, made fun constantly of Marian's poorly fitting and nearly threadbare clothing, and taunted him, though always from a distance and not long before they ran away. They called him *zlý pes*, a bad dog in Slovak, and Marian usually ignored them, until one day, when Tibor, the elder of the brothers, was alone and distracted, Marian (who had just emerged from a hiding place after reading one of his letters) took a stitching palm, reversed it on his hand so that the leather fit the outside of his knuckles, walked up to him, and punched him hard in the center of the chest. Tibor wobbled for a moment and then dropped to the ground. Marian removed the palm and threw it onto a nearby table, then took Tibor's good blanket-lined hunting coat off of him (it had been his dead father's) like one might undress a drunkard who had fallen asleep, and put it on. I stood by, wanting to see how this would all play out.

Marian buttoned the front of the coat, turned up the collar, and said to me, "*Čo myslíš, Jozef? Krásny, hej?*"

I told him that I'd never seen a finer coat, to which he nodded and said, "I'll need it for the mountains," although he had never been, and only heard my father speak obliquely of the flocks, the cabin, and the kind of work we did.

Tibor complained to his mother, who insisted that "that animal" give her son back his coat, but my father ignored her, and Tibor was afraid to fight and in time gave up his coat as a thing lost. After that, only my father ever called Marian by his Christian name. To everyone else, he was Zlee.

Which fit him better than even the coat, because something seemed to change in Zlee after he had tilted the balance of power there in the house, and he ventured out to see if it might work elsewhere, and began to look for fights, taking them on like an angry dog. He looked the part, too, with a loping stride like some Russian wolfhound, a gaze of regal and indifferent contentment on his face until he pounced, usually to avenge someone weaker who had no means of defending himself, but often enough simply to fight anyone who wore his strength like meanness on a sleeve, and then there was no way of escaping Zlee's lupine determination to stand and strike, until someone dropped and stayed down.

By the time Lent began, the villagers were grumbling and talking of running Zlee out of town (although he did have a strong advocate in a father whose simpleton daughter had wandered outside of the house one day and along the main road to the village store, where a couple of boys thought they might have some fun with her, until Zlee showed up, having been sent on an errand to buy flour). So, Zlee went with us into the mountains the following spring, as he had, in a way, foretold, and set right to the work of shepherding like a hired hand who'd been missed during a brief sabbatical but who had returned well rested and in form, and in time my father and I wondered how it was we had ever gotten along without him. And I don't know if the letters stopped coming, or if my father had stopped giving them to him, but Zlee never received another word from his mother, and he seemed to accept this turn away from one and toward another kind of life as one might accept a change of season.

IT SEEMS IMPOSSIBLE TO CONSIDER NOW, BUT AS I THINK BACK on that time, I was, like all the rest, afraid of Zlee that first winter he arrived. I wasn't sure who or what was behind the mask of the dog, and yet I can't say that I had any reason to believe that he'd turn on me. In the village, I shadowed him, mostly out of curiosity, but otherwise left him to himself, which he seemed to prefer. I was as intrigued as I was cautious of the way in which, seemingly without any effort or intent, wherever he walked or traveled or emerged, he became the center to which all things weakened or antagonistic were either drawn or from which they fled, and I wondered how long a man—a boy, rather—

could live this way until that center no longer held and the world he sought either to protect or punish broke apart before him and he was left to wander and search for a new world wherein nothing of the old one that had shaped him remained.

When my father took him into the mountains with us, though, I watched what I thought was that change come over Zlee. He accepted his role of novice to the husbandry we plied as a trade with an equanimity and gratitude, working side by side with me, asking for help and direction when he was given a task he hadn't done before, and my father acting as though it were unfolding all as he had planned. Perhaps it was. I could have led those flocks by myself, so well trained and used to that life had I become, but it had taken me some time to come into my own. And yet, by midsummer Zlee had picked up even the skills of shepherding that bordered on the instinctual (when to separate a ewe who had aborted; when milk would and wouldn't bring a lamb to thrive), as though having remembered them after a long time of toiling away at another kind of work, one that didn't suit him and clouded his sense of purpose, until someone told him to stop, brought him back to where he had begun, and placed in his hand an instrument he had never seen before but which he knew immediately he had been missing, and knew how to use.

The only time I ever saw Zlee caught off guard or seem in any way uncertain was when we had turned the first corner on the switchback that climbed for a good long mile on the path we had cut through the forest and up to the first of the springs where we and the animals watered, and my father told Zlee in English to tighten up the load that a new mule we had brought with us that season was carrying. He made no exceptions to his unwritten rule about the language we spoke once we left the village.

Zlee said, "Čo?"

And my father said again, "I want those girth straps tightened before we lose the whole damn load," and Zlee went silent.

I was out ahead but heard the exchange and so came back and cinched up the straps and repositioned the leather pad that kept them from digging into the mule's belly, and Zlee looked defeated somehow as he watched and translated my deliberate moves. But my father grinned and said in the only Slovak we would hear for the next seven months not to worry, that we never talked much in the mountains anyway, and Zlee took that to mean there was no harm done. By August, he was sitting down with us to read from Grant's memoirs, and listening tentatively as my father spoke in the voice of Ishmael about Ahab and the whale.

And while it seemed that he could do anything with a staff, a rope, or a knife in hand, of all the skills Zlee was asked to master that summer, he took to the rifle as though it were a language almost, for which he needed no grammar or tutoring or even alphabet, only ear and breath, which my father seemed to sense from the start, and which I never resented. I found hunting to be a skill I enjoyed honing, but it was more work than it was artistry for me, and had I not had the desire to focus on the details of the shot as much as I already had the desire to study and blend into all of nature surrounding, I might have been content with hunting only enough not to go hungry. Yet in Zlee, there was at his core something imperturbable, something his reputation as a tough who beat fools in order to be rid of them no doubt kept from the view of others (so that they might miscalculate the steady young man behind the bending frame), something that he unveiled there in the Carpathians, and which I witnessed as a transformation in him. The waiting and silence that came with shepherding and shooting both seemed to appeal to a natural discipline in Zlee that made him—and I say this from the distance of these many years—not part of man's world, but God's, so that as we worked and spoke and rested in silence, day after day and month after month, he became more like some contemplative seraph than a mere shepherd, a being at once willing and capable of defending what is good and beautiful and so moves easily and without disturbance from blithe to fearsome when the time comes to act.

WHY, THEN, AS I WATCHED WITH A KIND OF REVERENCE my brother's becoming, could I not see the arc of my father's fall?

He would not have described it as such, my father, but to me there was no other way to account for the slow loosening of the discipline he had himself impressed upon me, the views clung to (old and yet constantly put forth), which remained caught in their weak and circular rationale, and the growing resignation that his life—the life, that is, he took up after he returned from America—was meaningful only for the length of time he was given to atone for an incident deep in the past and as yet untold.

All of this played out on the level of the quotidian, imperceptible and harmless day after uneventful day, or so it seemed, until the pattern emerged.

Rather than being jostled awake in the morning (usually by Sawatch, sent to lick my face), I began rising before dawn to cook or begin the process of breaking camp, often finding Zlee already hard at it, while my father slept on and morning came and I had to strip him awake. In the daytime, as we moved from meadow to meadow, he left grazing decisions to me, which I took at first as a sign of confidence and still expected him to second-guess if there was something dangerous about the area that I couldn't see, but then realized (when it was Zlee and Sawatch who brought a cadre of lambs back from a steep ridge obscured by scrub pine) that he might not have cared if I led an entire flock of sheep over a cliff, and so I began to scout our moves more cautiously.

And at night, when our supper was over and there was little light to do anything but talk into the shadows— or rather, listen to my father's profile behind the candle while he gave the same tired ideas for problems universal and local—I thought nothing of the sweet plum smell of slivovica and the clear bottle that accompanied him on those evenings, until I started kicking empty ones at his bedside when it was time for all of us to be awake and moving.

The summer that I turned fifteen, my father returned from a trip to Kassa with extra rounds for the Krag, a .410 Hungarian-made shotgun, and a pair of Zeiss field glasses. We never wondered where he got the money to buy these things. They were tools, useful and necessary to us, like a sharp scythe necessary for harvest.

The .30-caliber rifle shells and nine-hundred-yard range of the Krag were too powerful for the rabbit and dove we ate plenty of in the mountains, but with the shotguns, Zlee and I not only kept up a steady supply of meat but also practiced our stalking skills, seeing how close we could get to unwary hares before we kicked up grass or tossed a stone to get them running, and then, after a head start, shot them with our Magyar blunderbuss.

Bullets for an American-made Krag were hard to come by in Europe, but my father didn't seem to have any trouble getting them through a connection he had in Kassa. We had little reason to fire the Krag often—practice and conditioning mostly—so he made only one trip a year to the city (the cultural center of what would become eastern Czechoslovakia) and its marketplace, where more than farmers plied their wares. That summer, though, my father restocked because we had gotten word that a mountain lion was giving trouble to some of the shepherds east of us and we knew it was only a matter of time before the big cat showed up in the hills surrounding Pastvina.

Those were the days when the last of the lions and pumas still roamed the Tatras and Carpathians, and in late August we started to find fresh kills on the periphery of the herd, usually a lamb or two, but often enough one of the ewes. If that predator had only taken the weak and moved on, nature doing the culling we ourselves would have done, we'd have let her have her share. But she seemed to hunt with a bloodlust, and we couldn't afford to lose the horse or mule, or, worse, find one of us face-to-face with her as we came up a switchback.

My father began going down to Eperjes every other week then. In the town square, where the farmers set up stalls and sold their produce, there was talk of "*levica*," the lioness, sometimes with awe, sometimes with contempt, as though she were goddess and succubus in one body, and my father would return and give us these reports, and at night, under the spell of his brandy, he began telling us more and more about America and the mountains of Colorado, where there were lions, too, but they were remote animals and remained in the higher altitudes, away from men. And then he said (the pronouncement strange, for his voice spoke to neither Zlee nor me), "but they will find you when the time comes."

He began carrying the rifle with him—on horseback, on foot, in his bed. I asked him why he thought he'd run into the cat in broad daylight or asleep in the cabin, and he asked me when it was I had gotten so smart, and I let him be. But I could tell that he was beyond cautious or even superstitious of the cat's presence. He was somehow thrown off, as though he hadn't expected such an adversary to encroach on his mountain pastoral. Or worse, that her presence meant she had come to the end of a long game of stalking and the hunt was about to be finished.

One morning before first light we heard the hard bleating of a ewe in distress and my father was outside and moving fast through the flock before Zlee and I even knew what was happening. I heard a shot as I came out of the door of the cabin, and another as I broke into a run. When I reached my father, he was holding the barrel high and staring off into the light rising in the east.

There was barely enough dawn to see, but if my father had pulled a trigger—and twice—I believed there was reason, and so I asked breathlessly, "Did you get her?"

"I don't know," he said.

"Let's follow the blood. Which direction did she run in?"

"I don't know," he said again, scaring me a little.

"You don't know?" I asked, more out of disbelief than anything.

"For Christ's sake, Jozef. I said I don't know."

We were silent for some time, and I listened to the mauled ewe suck air (she had fought in what way she could, big and strong as she was) and kick at the hard ground with her hooves, until she stopped kicking and breathing altogether and lay in her bed of grass and gore.

Two days later, we buried Sawatch in a shade of pines to the back of the cabin and went inside without a word. My father began packing food (what looked like enough for three days) into a rucksack, threw four rounds into a side pocket, took the Krag down from the wall and handed it to Zlee, then gave me the rucksack and a leather case with the field glasses inside.

"I was up all night figuring this, even while that thing was killing my dog," he said. "She's hunting from the top of Krížik Ridge. Has to be. I want you boys to come back with most of those rounds and enough food for a guest. I don't even want to see that cat."

Zlee and I took a lame ram we were going to have to put down anyway, hiked the whole day up to the ridge— the highest point just above the tree line there in that part of the mountains, Krížik was named for the crosslike shape it resembled, with a long horizontal cave that rested on the top of a towering shaft of granite—left the ram on the trail and found a thick stand of birch about 250 yards away and upwind, where we sat hidden, waiting.

The ram brayed, tried to run, grazed on some low-growing thistle, and then slept. We spent the night listening and resting in shifts. I glassed the ridge at sunrise but didn't see a thing. We watched all morning and into the afternoon, then left our cover and walked the ram back down into a meadow, clearing the air before we tried again the next night. Nothing. Three days we spent observing that ridge, until I woke up the next morning and saw Zlee standing to take in the view of the valley behind us and a slice of the distant range visible from our blind.

"Your father's wrong," he said. "That lion's not here. And if she was, she's not coming back here, at least not to hunt anything tied down."

We had run out of food, so, disappointed as I was that we wouldn't get the cat, I was glad we'd be heading back to our camp, and I said to Zlee, "Do you mean in the mountains, or not here on this ridge?"

"I mean not where we are," he said. "If this lion's hunting, why do we believe that we can leave some old animal in her path and expect her to show up for us? We're not tracking a creature of habit. She's stayed alive in these mountains for a long time by doing more than stalking sheep."

I told him I understood, and that we should take the ram back to the camp, reprovision ourselves, and try again in another place.

"Jozef, don't you see?" His eyes flashed, lightless as it was, and I don't think he had slept at all. That lion had picked through the best of the flock, he said, not the weak and the lame, but the strong, and she was going to keep on hunting for one better prize after another. "And all we've done is wait for her, and fired into the air at her shadow. But if we could find her, without her seeing us, while she stalks, we just might be able to kill her. There's no other way."

We tethered the ram to a stake at the mouth of a thrum-cap overhang. Then, our packs empty, we set off for the valley where my father said that he was taking the sheep for some protection until we returned, a day's hike from there.

It was dusk when we arrived. I still remember looking down on him from the brow of a hill we had just come over. He was scanning the perimeter of those same hills rising out of the valley in which he and his sheep had lain down for the night, but he didn't see us, just turned his back and set to the chores of the evening, slowly and with a break every now and then when he'd sit and stare at the ground, not, it seemed, because he was tired but, rather, as though he had forgotten what it was he needed to do next. I felt the wind coming up out of the mountains from the northeast.

We had approached on purpose in a long sweep from the west. I carried the Krag, while Zlee scouted ahead and found a group of large boulders midway up the hill, and we nestled in behind them. They covered our backs and gave us a good view of the surrounding terrain. I had watched my father from a distance before and he had always somehow seen me without my knowing. Now, with no idea that Zlee and I were there, he seemed fragile and alone as he finished setting up his small tent, built a fire, and warmed his soup. I felt alone, too. I wanted to go to him, listen to him talk as he stirred what would be our supper, or hear him read, and be a boy again there in the mountains.

Zlee and I hadn't eaten all day, but we didn't speak of food. We communicated in signs and short sentences, the last of which was when he shook me awake before dawn, held a finger to his lips for silence and handed me the field glasses.

"Four hundred yards," he whispered, and I saw the brown-and-silvery figure threading past makeshift pens of sleeping sheep. How was it that nothing stirred? By some power or invisibility, the lion stalked along steadily, and I could tell that she was through with killing sheep.

It crossed my mind, briefly, to ask Zlee if he wanted to take the shot, but the movement involved in the very act of turning and questioning might be discernible to the cat. So I settled into my breathing, and the only other words Zlee spoke were a short comment on the growing light, and wind, which I took to mean that I hadn't much time.

I thought of my father, who was sleeping soundly below, not knowing what lay in store for him if I missed. He would be rising soon, and I suspect the cat was waiting for when her prey would emerge from the tent and move away from the protective cover of canvas. I had one shot. The sky was brightening in that way morning seems to come on all at once in the summer, and I waited, holding the animal's haunch in my sight. I eased the barrel slightly right, took one full breath and could smell the faint musk of the well-oiled gun stock mingling with my own unbathed stench, and almost sighed as I pulled the trigger. The shot's echo seemed to crack open the valley, and the cat, as though powering in that direction, slumped to one side.

WHEN WE WENT BACK DOWN TO PASTVINA FOR THE WINTER in 1914, all we heard was talk of the war. Boys a few years older than I wore their cadet uniforms daily, and men from our village marched off to the conscription office in Eperjes to join the fight against the Russians on the eastern front. There was a fever rising, and not just for battle. Young men, as always, sensed a chance to leave the boredom of their villages and see to the borders of the empire and beyond, but this time their departure was imminent, and so they lived and worked and moved in a tension between excitement and rage. Or maybe I'm just remembering what the thoughts of war began to evoke in me.

I never felt at home there in the village, the close-packed houses, the lack of privacy, the sense, as I grew to be a young man, that my father was seen as a failure or a kind of fool. His wife, who must have sensed the man's declining confidence, berated him endlessly about money, and his stepsons acted as though they were the men of the house, when they were nothing more than layabouts. I even saw it when we went to the shop along the main street of the village. No one greeted my father or asked him how the summer had treated him in the mountains. Not so much as *"Dobrý deň."* He was, indeed, a man who appeared as though he had come down off a mountain and yet seemed weaker, somehow less a man among other men as a result of it. And I wanted to grab those people and cuff them for their ignorance, hold them by the neck and make them kneel before my father, but when I turned to him, looking for and expecting to see in him— for my sake—something of the man I knew, who had shaped me, he seemed, year after year, to shrink before us all, as though somehow the streets and houses and vil-lagers we walked among now reminded him of not just a humility but a weakness waiting to inhabit him, and it was his duty to relent.

My stepbrothers were doing their mandatory cadet service that year and were waiting to be conscripted into the Honvéd in the spring. By December, they moved about the house with a kind of recklessness. I saw it in others, too, just boys who knew there was something larger than they could imagine happening hundreds of miles to the east and west of us, something that in all like-lihood, once they were a part of it, would destroy them.

But my stepmother's sons, who mistook her coddling for belief in their natural superiority, became nothing more than spoiled thugs. I despised them, especially Tibor. Both of them were bug-eyed and fleshy, which was a rare thing in that part of the world, because there wasn't that much food or time to be idle. But their mother fed them constantly, as she had done from childhood, kept them from work, and filled their heads with the notion that they deserved more and would receive more once they found their opportunity to leave Pastvina and claim the greatness that was rightfully theirs.

That January, I was in the barn, replacing a board on an old cart we used for transporting the wooden boxes of bryndza. It was cold, but I had to saw and plane pinewood to shape and so I worked without a coat on. I heard someone come into the barn and I looked up, expecting to find Zlee, because I had asked him for help and was wondering why he had forgotten. Then I saw Tibor and Miro standing in front of me. It wasn't quite noon, but they were drunk, and from that short distance I could smell on their breaths the homemade slivovica they had stolen from my father's cellar.

"Look at Jozef," Tibor said to Miro. "Strong enough to work in this cold as though it were summer in the mountains." He took a long drag on the cigarette he was smoking, exhaled, dropped the fag on the dirt floor, and left it to smolder.

I said, "Isn't there work of your own you two need to do?" and turned back to planing the side of that board. And before I could tell what was happening, Miro grabbed me and punched me twice in the stomach, the shock and pain of the blow doubling me over, so that I fell and couldn't move.

"That's for Tibor's coat," he said, as though it had happened yesterday.

Miro was even fatter than his brother, not the smarter of the two, and he pinned me down while Tibor came over and started to tie my wrists and ankles together with a length of rope. Every time I tried to push or kick free, Miro pummeled me. When all I could think to do was to spit on him, he punched me in the stomach again and picked me up and threw me over a sawhorse.

I heard Tibor hiss, "*I'm first*," and I made one last kick to free myself, but Miro brought his pulpy fist into the side of my head. "Isn't this how you do it at your sheep camp, Jozef?" Tibor panted, the alcohol on his breath the only thing keeping me from passing out.

Then I heard Zlee's voice, slow and full-toned as it was. "Tibor, you pig!"

The brothers could not have felt anything but fear. Miro turned and rushed at Zlee, and Zlee landed a punch so hard to the center of Miro's chest that he seemed to shoot upright and gasp for breath all in one motion. Then Zlee brought his knee up into Miro's crotch and I heard a crack and a strange squeaking sound. I rolled off the wooden horse and, in a daze, saw Tibor run to the back of the barn.

"You, you s-stay away from me, Pes," he said.

Zlee backed him into a stall and hit him hard in the midsection, first one punch, then another, each one knocking more wind out of him, until he collapsed. Then, working as methodically as though these were animals he had come to feed, Zlee stuffed a fistful of hay into Tibor's mouth, grabbed his arm, and bent it back until it snapped. Tibor screamed and Zlee shoved another fistful of hay into his face.

I came to my senses on the ground, kicking against the ropes while Zlee untied me, and my voice rose through anger and pain. "Let me kill him!" I said.

But Zlee told me to hold still, untied me, wiped blood from my lip with a handkerchief that smelled of lye soap and said, "No. It's over. Let's go. You hurt them now and it's prison with the real pigs. They've got worse coming."

But rage welled in me and I shook off Zlee, stood up, grabbed a pitchfork propped in a corner, and walked over to Tibor, who lay whimpering in the frozen shit and mud of that empty stall. I raised the tines above my head and summoned all of the strength I could to drive them through his body. And I would have if Zlee hadn't taken it from me and set it down as I held my head in my hands and wept.

"Let's go," he said again. "We need to tell your father about this before he finds them and they give him a story." And we walked back into the house, where my father was writing letters by the stove.

I don't know if it's a punishment or meant for some other purpose, but if there is a God, He has seen to it that I should remember every face that has ever looked at or spoken to me. And yet of all the faces that crowd my memory, I can still see the face of Miro as we passed him on the way out of the barn that morning. It appears like a short series of pictures: His knees are drawn up and he's holding his legs and hiccupping for air, when he suddenly looks at me, reaches out his hand, and tries to plead with me to help him, as though the young man that bore his likeness minutes before has been transformed, leaving only an innocent caught up in a fight he doesn't understand, and unable to make a sound.

But when we told my father that Tibor and Miro were hurt and in the barn after they had tried to beat me for some long-held grudge, he became angry, said that those two were just nervous about their induction and that at heart they were good boys who didn't know any better. "How bad are they?" he asked.

"*Otec*," Zlee said, calling him "Father," just as I did, "they were trying to—"

I cut him off. "No, Zlee."

"Marian," my father asked again, his voice rising and impatient now. "How bad are they?"

"*Vel'mi zlý*," he replied.

"Goddamn it!" My father brought his fist down on the table and began to shout at us there in the kitchen, telling Zlee that he was tired of the fighting and stories of beatings that followed him everywhere he went. "There'll come a time when I won't be able to protect you any longer, and I'm not even sure that I'll want to," he said, though we all knew that he was incapable of protecting even himself anymore. "Go and get the doctor, and we'll see what comes of this."

Nothing came of it. Miro and Tibor left for the war together in the summer of 1915 and were sent to fight in Galicia, in spite of Tibor's poorly set arm. Sometime in the fall, we got preprinted postcards, which every soldier on the front initialed and sent home before battle. Then, in the winter, the only villager who ever returned to us from the east alive (he had lost a leg and spoke with a quaver in his voice) told us that Tibor had been shot and killed point-blank in the trench by his commanding officer for refusing to attack when ordered. Miro was killed in a wave of shelling by the Russians, blown in half, this man who fought in their company said, but taking some time to die as his legless trunk of a body lay against the stump of a fallen tree and he clawed at the sky, pleading for someone to help him. Their mother believed they had died heroes, and no one saw any reason to tell her otherwise. She gave all the money she had to the priest, who said Masses for their souls. And yet when I heard about their deaths, I wished I had killed them, carrying that rage within me like an animal tied down and caged, and I prayed for the war to last, though I still had a year to go.

That night, my mother came to me in a dream again. Her face seemed no longer radiant, as it had been when I was a boy, but, rather, etched with sadness. No, not sadness. Fear. The look of fear. I know, because I saw that look everywhere. And while I wondered what it was she was afraid of, and even began to feel it rising in me, she spoke for the first time. Her arms outstretched, as they always were, she said, "*Lúbim t'a*," words of love from a mother to a son, and I reached out for her, wanting her to speak again, to tell me *why*, and to remain there so that I might know something of who she was, if she did, in fact, love me, as she said. But her image fluttered and shook, and when I awoke, the solace I had felt from her in the past comfort of those dreams had been replaced by a hard and intractable anger.

Ash Wednesday came in mid-February in 1915, and from the day we set out in late winter of that year on the trail that took us from the village into the mountains, the skies threatening and the path already buried in snow, if I wasn't quiet and sullen enough to ignore all but the simplest requests made of me, I took to arguing with my father's opinions, regardless of where I stood on them. He'd look dismayed, and then disdainful, until we just stopped talking, or until Zlee brought up the weather.

My father was against the war. He was convinced that it was only a matter of time before the Americans came in on the side of the English and French, which would mean the end of Germany and Austria-Hungary. But few people in Pastvina, or any of the other surrounding villages, could read anything beyond the Hungarian the few years of state school gave them, and all of the papers printed in Kassa and Budapest praised the emperor and his unmatched, loyal army, reporting only the victories we achieved against hapless Russians and now the Italians, who outnumbered us. Even as more and more food, men, and morale disappeared.

He hadn't hatched these ideas on his own. Along with supplies we needed at the camp, my father also managed to bring back from his trips to Kassa a few black-market back issues of *The New York Times* and *The Manchester Guardian*. These were meant to be part of our English lessons, but they also shaped his view that the Habsburg dynasty had reached its twilight and was about to be snuffed out. My father was convinced that the problem of the Slavs, as they referred to the conflicts that kept rising up out of every corner of the empire, was the one thing Ferdinand might have reformed. His wife was even a Czech. And then he was assassinated—by a Slav.

"The problem of the Slavs is the Slavs themselves," my father would say when our debates turned to whether Russia's revolution was a force of good or just another struggle that would benefit a few and leave the peasants starving. Then he would pick up a book from his precious shelf of works in English, heft it, and say, depending on whom he felt like reading, "We need a Grant" or "We need a Lincoln, not a Trotsky."

That was how we passed most spring and summer nights that year, exhausted in the candlelight of our cabin from the work we did, while the animals we shepherded ate or slept along the hills outside and boys marched off to war from their families and farms below. Until I got it into my head that the man who had raised me, and all his views, were the ridiculous and subversive rantings of a drunken coward and it was time that I rejected them.

When Zlee turned eighteen in March 1916 and had to register at the conscription office in Eperjes, I had a printer in the city alter my identity card so I could join up early, and I went to present my papers along with all those who were of fighting age. In any other year, they might have balked, checked, and sent me home to wait, but the Honvéd were so desperate for conscripts that it turned a blind eye when Zlee said to the officer in charge, "He's from the mountains, sir, and can shoot." That was all they needed. I passed my physical and was told to report back in two days, ready for basic training.

And so, it was on the eve of my departure to fight for the Austro-Hungarian army in the Great War—a night I spent with my father down off the mountain (he had paid the Rusyn peasants to watch his flocks for two days), in spring, so that, as we walked into the village at midday, the green grass and fruit tree blossoms and din of children's voices and animals who had given birth in the barnyards that were attached to houses like second rooms seemed the stage of some play I happened upon and watched from behind a curtain—that my father told me all that he remembered about the day my mother died over the Arkansas River in Pueblo, Colorado, and why it was we left America for the old country.

"I stopped believing a long time ago," he said into the

darkness, against which we had lit a single candle, "but that doesn't mean, like any unbeliever, that I might not be mistaken. You see, I felt the conviction that some judgment had been passed down by God, and the others who said they feared this God, so that if I didn't somehow atone for what I'd failed to do, after losing everything, I'd lose the only person I'd ever loved in this world. You."

In the morning, he waited for me by the door, kissed me on the forehead, whispered into my ear, "*Lúbim t'a*," and we parted.

ZLEE AND I WERE LUCKY TO HAVE JOINED UP TOGETHER. Basic training, with its weeks of constant drilling from dawn well into the night, seemed a thing requiring no effort. We were used to a life of early mornings and physical labor outside all day. It knocked us down a few pegs, got us used to hearing obscenities for marching sloppily or wearing scuffed boots, or maybe it was just to remind us that there was someone whose job it was to tell us what to do every waking hour of those days, and I began to miss the leisure of books and conversation, but I confronted these obstacles as a simple rite of passage. And Zlee, Zlee had this way—maddening to our corporal, who had never seen battle, and would likely have turned tail if he had—of conforming to the least detail with obsessive perfection, all the while making it clear by his indifferent, canine stride and aloof, unanimated face that these least details (which he would see to their completion) meant nothing to him. Zlee was as indomitable as he was bereft of guile.

But it wasn't until the final weeks, when we began to practice on the rifle range, that our fate, you might say, was sealed, when the training officer discovered that we really could shoot.

Conditions on those firing ranges were ideal—no reflecting sun, no tree branches, no animals bolting when you got a bead on them. The only thing we weren't used to were the Steyr Mannlicher rifles we fired, standard infantry issue in the army of the empire. They were thin top-bolt rifles with a five-clip magazine, one of the first of their kind. They had a strong kick and could jam easily when exposed to dirt, but we didn't have to worry about any of this yet. It took the two of us a few rounds to sight them, and after that, on the twenty-five-yard range, Zlee and I hit ten out of ten bull's-eyes, dead center, some of the rounds piled up on top of one another. The other conscripts barely raised dirt around those targets.

At first, we were assigned, along with all the others who mustered in Eperjes, to General Kray's command. Kray was a Napoleonic Hungarian who led a brigade made up of Slovak march batallions, which meant that we'd be fighting with men who shared not only a common language but the experience of daily life, ritual, and labor. Kray's soldiers were known for being good fighters because they worked the land and weren't soft, and I had a deep sense of having done the right thing, feeling as though I had been called somehow to take leave of my father and Pastvina and to prove myself in the world.

Then, at the end of our basic training, Zlee and I were pulled from the ranks without explanation and led into a tent where a captain sat behind a desk made up of two trunks with a board laid across the top. He was Austrian, which was evident by his uniform, and spoke to us in a bookish-sounding Hungarian. He wore black boots that had a soft, worn gloss to them, and he fiddled with a riding crop.

"So, you are from one of Kray's regiments," he said, and began to pace behind his station and question us about our village, our parents, how it was we had learned to shoot so well. He seemed intrigued by Zlee's insistence that he was an orphan adopted by my father and that we were brothers not of blood but of labor and the land.

"Labor," he said. "You sound like a Communist. Don't all mothers labor to bear their sons in blood?"

Zlee said that he had never met a Communist and so couldn't say what one sounded like. What he meant was that he and I were as close as brothers because of the life my father had given us both. "Sir, I have seen him work on the land, and so I know what this Soldat will do in battle," Zlee said, staring straight ahead as he spoke of me as a Soldat, which I was, all the while maintaining the soldier's respect for his superior and never once making eye contact with that captain, who cursed and spat and said, "You know nothing of battle."

Then he turned to me. "*Und Sie*," he said. "*Was haben Sie über diese Bruderschaft zu sagen?*"

I don't know why he switched to his native language then, but I knew enough German to understand that he wanted to know what I thought of this brotherhood Zlee spoke of. The summer before I signed up, I had studied the standard commands of the army so that I wouldn't be turned away if they questioned me, and the language came easily. Could he have known this? Could he have known, too, that Zlee's German didn't go beyond twenty or so words because he had no head for anything that required study, from a book, that is? No, this captain was testing my loyalty—it was plain to me—wanting to see how I would respond if I was given a chance to speak privately. And so, thinking not in German but in a foreign language I knew, I replied in English, "Sir, there is nothing my father taught me that he didn't teach him also."

The captain looked surprised, smiled, and asked Zlee, "How is your English, Private Pes?"

Zlee, still staring doggedly at some point on the wall, said, "Sir, better than you might expect."

A few days later, just before the entire battalion was supposed to move out, we were released from our regiment, given lance corporal stars to attach to our uniform collars, and boarded a train with a company of other soldiers going in the same direction, but not the same place.

That night, we arrived at a camp on the Duna outside of Pozsony. A sergeant barked orders at us there in the dark, where we stood at attention for what seemed like hours, until two officers showed up, and the sergeant snapped to attention himself and then receded. One, another Austrian captain, did all the talking, while the other, whose uniform was German but whose overcoat looked more like some Bavarian hunter's, stood by, listening and surveying us there in the harsh light.

Nineteen sixteen was the year the Austrians started sending sharpshooters to learn sniping skills for the front. Most of these schools recruited men from the Tirolean region of the Southern Alps, on the border with Italy, and were run by German officers. Scharfschützen, they called them. The Italians called them cecchini and (we were to learn in time) feared them more than anything else in those mountains. Under that veil of mock secrecy, it emerged that we were being sent to a place in Austria called Klagenfurt to be trained as Scharfschützen for the empire's defense of its culture and threatened borders on the southern front. We had been chosen, the captain told us, not only for our marksmanship but for our character and ability to endure hardship in conditions under which most men would buckle, although I'm sure he knew or cared nothing about my character. The emperor himself understood who we were and how important our mission was, he said to us, and from there on out we were ordered never to speak unless spoken to by a superior officer, and any soldier showing the least amount of weakness or lack of discipline and restraint would be sent straight back to his regiment and a trench on the eastern front.

There we were, forty of us, men from the ranks—although there were only four other Slavs, two Bosnians, and two Czechs—brought together because we had a common skill that was about to be pressed into service. I didn't understand what it meant then to have what the captain referred to as a gift. There were plenty of Front-kämpfer, he said, the frontline infantry, who wore the marksman's badge and would line up in the trenches next to machine gunners when the enemy attacked. We weren't riflemen, though. We weren't Frontkämpfer. We were hunters who already knew how to stalk game in the mountains and forests we had lived in before the war, and who were now being taught to hunt men, observing their numbers, their movements, their skills or the lack of them, their habits, and ultimately their faces—front or back—through the crosshairs of a rifle scope, all so that we might kill them, one at a time, with a silence that terrified them more than anything because it held nothing of the glory they imagined they'd find in battle.

In Klagenfurt, we trained and practiced—not just drilled but practiced—as though virtuosi who would one day be given their concert hall solos in some great symphonic concerto, conducted by our maestro, Sergeant Major Bücher, who had been fighting on the western front since August 1914, until he lost a leg to a long-range French shell that had caught him leaving the line at Verdun. He limped well enough with the prosthetic limb a puppet maker in Leipzig had carved for him, but the Germans were one sharpshooter down at the front as a result. So he offered his services as an instructor and would always say, as we stood at attention at dawn on snow-packed and frozen ground while he paced before us, that the sharpshooter should consider himself above rank and disregard it, as it is rank that ought to be hunted first, killing from the top down in order to leave an army leaderless and demoralized. Search for whom and what seems out of the ordinary, he instructed us. The nonuniform, the affectation. Field glasses around the neck out in the open. A scarf of school colors catching the wind. A knitted pullover. An umbrella.

"To desire rank is to desire death," he intoned aphoristically. "You must find the soldier of rank, and find in yourselves the will to remain calm, silent, and alert. Then kill as though it were your only chance to live."

For the first week, we never fired a shot. We cleaned our rifles six times a day and became familiar with the meticulous care of optical sights. We learned to read maps and draw maps and study maps taken from prisoners, so that we could see our ground from their perspective. We dressed in white cover to blend in with the snow during those late-winter months and practiced Nordic techniques until we could ski fifteen miles with a thirty-pound pack on our backs and not fall. We learned how to range, judge distances, take into account variations of topography, spot and report small troop movement, and how to move instinctively—against the instincts of the average man—toward higher ground there in the Alps, while we sought out a good hide, and a good means of escape. That was, Bücher said, if we knew and could

employ well the full quiver of our skills, the most important weapon we could find, a safe place to hide, and this
exercise made up the second week of our training.

Each day, we disappeared into the woods, wanting to
see and not be seen. Most of us they had chosen in twos,
and so we worked in twos, Zlee and I seemingly insepara-
ble now as spotter and shooter. After we were dismissed
into the forests in teams, the remaining men fanned out to
find us, just as my father and I had done in the mountains
years ago, hunter and hunted making notes on details of
an occupied position, until the hunter ultimately revealed
his target. If the hunted—watching from the hide—had
more information on the hunter, the teams switched roles.
The one with better notes got the kill. Sometimes it was as
insignificant as the fold in a man's cap.

Zlee and I started out against a pair of Tiroleans from
the Landesschützen, severe and insular men of the Alpine
regions who had remained loyal to the Habsburgs. They
kept to themselves and seemed especially derisive of the
standard Austrian officers. They hated Slavs, too. It didn't
matter that we were fighting for the same king.

We found them easily enough because they whispered
to each other in their mountain dialect as they hid in the
socket of two large boulders, which created a kind of
sounding board. They must have thought we couldn't
hear them if we couldn't understand them, and so they
cursed us when Zlee inched his head over the top of the
rock, looked down, and said in a whisper, "*Boom.*" I had
a page of notes on them, even jotting down a word I
transliterated from their Austrian, which Bücher knew I
could not have known, and he called them "useless jokers," and sent them back to their regiment. Once Zlee
and I were given the chance to disappear, no one found

us, not even Bücher, who had his own perch with a tele-
scope, from which he made notes—good ones, too.

It was just as well that we couldn't be found, because,
but for the sergeant major's attention, we were ignored.
The men we trained with were mostly Austrians, and the
training we got was unique to the man sent to instruct us.
In spite of Bücher's insistence that the best weapon the
empire had was the men who lived and survived in her
mountains, captains who did the recruiting chose as
sharpshooters young Austrian men who knew the luxury
of sport hunting and who arrived in Klagenfurt with their
own rifles, like gentlemen showing up at school with their
own horses. That's where I saw my first Schoenauer, a
beautiful and powerful rifle with the precision of a surgi-
cal instrument. I saw the Norwegian model of the Krag,
German Mausers and Gewehr 98s sent down from the
western front, and a few other peculiar cannons that looked
as though they should have been left in the nineteenth
century. But the weapon didn't make the shot, and in the
end more than a few of those gentlemen were sent home
with their rifles, where they'd live to hunt game-park
deer, not Italian soldiers.

Twenty-five of us remained by the third week, and
that's when we took to the range again, this time firing a
long-barrel Mannlicher 95 with a double-set trigger and
fitted with an optical sight, the physical effect of which
was still something new for Zlee and me, despite the fact
that we had been carrying them around and caring for
them for weeks. We were trained to make head shots and
aimed for the teeth, which seems ludicrous until, on a
cold morning, across the distance of a valley through
refracted light, you can suddenly see a man's breath, see
that he's speaking to a comrade, or perhaps only to him-

self, having a smoke, singing a song he loves, or maybe giving voice to some prayer, words that will be his last. It was hand-to-hand combat, except that the enemy never saw your hand, and lifted his to no effect.

As a team with rifle, rounds, field glasses, and maps, Zlee and I were a rarity, spotter and shooter equally good at both. Bücher called us *die Zwillinge,* "the twins." And then, almost as quickly as it began, just shy of a month of training in that mountain forest by the lake and on ground soft and thawing in the sun, we were pronounced ready, given gold-colored sharpshooter cords for our uniforms, told to keep silent and alert, and sent off to the front, unaware of what kind of war awaited us there.

LIKE MOST OF THE TROOPS ON THAT TRAIN, MEN WHO STRODE along the ravines and through forests from Ljubljana west to the river town of Most na Soči, Zlee and I had yet to see battle, and we were a spirited, if tentative, bunch, some men singing, others shouting boastful taunts to unseen and unknown Italians, until, idle and waiting at the station platforms of small and emptied Slovenian towns, we saw our first trains of the wounded push past.

Closer to the lines, we came upon the field hospitals and casualty-clearing stations, where the lives of those men in all their misery were born.

Because this was where trains were constantly switching, we stopped and were held there, which must have been some mistake if anyone had the morale of new soldiers in mind. Some joked, others praised the valor of the wounded, but most of us just looked away or made the sign of the cross to hide our unease, unease at the sight of figures prone on stretchers or laid out on the frozen ground, some screaming and crying for their mothers like hurt children, others emitting a rhythm of slow moans, as though their breath had to pass through the reed of a bassoon. Some never uttered a sound. Soldiers old enough to have facial hair at that time wore their best imitations of Franz Jozef's handlebar mustache. On the gray and emaciated lips of the dying, though, those mustaches appeared unkempt and spindling imitations of the real thing.

I don't know how many hours we waited, or for what or whom we were waiting. Trains that had arrived behind us had inched out of there long ago. It seemed an eternity passing and chipping away at our collective desire at that moment to hurl our young wills into what battle awaited us, believing somehow that we would be saved and emerge unscathed, while others, though lost, should live on in our memories as heroes, so that the borders our train approached might remain drawn as though time itself had drawn them.

From the siding, we could hear long-range artillery dropping randomly in the distance, indistinguishable from the thunder of a storm passing, or commencing. One stretcher would get ferried into a tent, while others still waited outside, the look on the ones left behind, if they looked at all, an aspect of dismay and surprise. I watched a young woman without expression on a face that might once have been pretty carrying a large bucket like it was just another basin of wash water, the bucket pressed against an apron soaked in blood. She stopped beside a cistern I hadn't noticed before (or, if I had, couldn't recognize what its contents were) and dumped her care of body parts into a swill of larger limbs. On her way back to the tent, she leaned over one of the silent, mustached officers, who looked as though he had fallen asleep, and pulled the dirty wool blanket that had accompanied him to these grounds over his face. Then she disappeared.

And at about the time I saw the sun dropping through a break in the clouds to the west, the conductor whistled that we were to depart, and the company commander shouted at a group of men who were smoking and had started a game of cards, so that some brushed their winnings into their hats and they all swung aboard as the train lurched, and we were off, not stopping again on that pilgrimage from which most of us would never return, until we had reached the front.

EXCEPT FOR THE INTERMITTENT EXERCISE OF ARTILLERY RANGing or harassing, the Soča Valley was quiet in the early spring of 1917. There had been many defeats the year before, but our army held the hills to the north, east, and south of Görz and could survey the Italian lines more strategically than if the city had remained in Austrian hands. Zlee and I knew nothing of battles won and lost along this river in the months and years before we'd arrived. Apart from the dead and wounded we had seen as we approached, the grounds seemed fixed and ordered to us, with trenches dug from rock and sandbagged higher, gun placements set up forward of and behind the lines (as though monstrous men themselves who would move into and out of battle at a general's command), and all of this wending its way around the outlying hills of that town through which the Soča flowed, a town that, when I glassed it for the first time, seemed a place too old and delicate and beautiful to be the center of so much destruction.

Nothing of this appeared as I'd expected war to appear, although, in truth, I can't say if I had a vision of war in mind, save perhaps for the placement of men who were wont to fight. I expected open fields and open ground, where columns of the emperor's soldiers in pike gray marched in place, broke for the charge, and clashed, until the strong defeated the weak on that ground. But the only surface that was wide and open in this land was the river herself, which flowed serene and cottony blue, while entire armies hid themselves and their weapons and woke each day and watched and waited for the other to move or show himself above the top of each other's subterranean world.

Zlee and I were attached to a regiment dug in north of Görz and, having survived the roulette of artillery and trench mortars in that first week, were itching for some action. Well fed (at the time), kitted out with good woolen uniforms, and fit, we brushed off the scene we had glimpsed at the field hospital, as well as rumors we heard that our army was barely holding on against an Italian onslaught. Up and down the lines, while men continued to dig and strengthen trenches that had literally been hewn out of rock, they spoke of General Boroević as though he were their father, or their god.

"Sveto won't give them Trieste," they'd say. Or "Boroević could have Görz back tomorrow if he wanted it." I never met the man, but it was a comfort to me that so many soldiers, in the ranks and among the officers, believed in him as a commander.

It was after stand-to at dusk one day that we were told by a captain to report immediately to Major Márai's tent. Though we were only lance corporals, as sharpshooters we reported to Márai, who reported directly to Colonel Rhelen, whom we rarely saw, which didn't matter. Sharpshooters were given freedom to range along the lines in search of good targets in spite of our regimental assignment because that was what the Germans did, so that's what our Austrian commanders let us do. We were lone hunters among the other officers and ordinary ranks of infantry, and this set us apart, sometimes with awe, most times with contempt, especially among the sergeants and first lieutenants, whose jobs were to maintain discipline and order in their platoons. We wore the identifying lanyard on the outside of our uniforms, carried a rifle with an optical sight and a barrel longer than the average soldier's carbine, and always traveled in twos. If these weren't enough to tip off whichever captain wanted to know why we were separated from our unit, we simply replied, "*Scharfschützen, Herr Hauptmann.*"

Yet we were welcomed by the veterans of the Soča because they saw firsthand why it was we listened and spoke to no one, and knew that in the balance of power our success raised the likelihood that they'd remain alive one more day. In those battlements, natural and man-made, the Austrians maintained a state of readiness throughout most of the winter. There was constant talk of yet another Italian offensive, which we would have to wait for, as we didn't have enough reserves to launch one ourselves, and that lethal mix of rumor and readiness wore on a soldier's nerves. But because our orders were to carve away at the long vast body that made up the Italian lines one limb and member at a time, we boosted morale when forward units saw us moving through a trench past them, or a sentry gave word in the morning after stand-to that a team of sharpshooters was in the sector.

And so, that evening we were told to rest and ready our weapon, and by midnight we were hidden and silent

and waiting in an abandoned kaverne with an escape
route through a tunnel out the back.

MY FIRST KILL WAS A MEMBER OF THE BERSIGLIERI, THE ELITE
Italian infantry, though to me he was just a solider who
got as close as possible to the forward line on motorcycle
and then marched several hundred yards carrying a
leather pouch toward a manned trench. Zlee spotted him
when he was still on his bike, which made one hell of a
racket in the quiet dawn. From our position, and according to orders, we had been expecting only to report on
movement that day, but there seemed an arrogance to this
man, his arrival, his singular message, the ridiculous cap he
wore, which had something like plumage sticking from the
top of it, and the rage that I had carried to this war found
itself focused. From where we stood behind our shield of
rock and dirt, the front was two hundred yards away. I had
the man in my sights from the moment Zlee said, "Moving
target, five hundred yards." I'll lose him when he ducks
into a dugout, I thought, but he marched right up and
stood in a part of their trench that rose to his shoulders and
left his neck and head exposed. I aimed for his ear, just
below that goddamn peacock's head of a helmet he wore,
and pulled the trigger.

"That's a kill," Zlee said as I watched the man's profile disappear, the first life I had ever taken.

I bolted another round, held, and waited. There was
scrambling and someone yelled *Cecchini!* A face rose
in that same position, this time looking right at me
through the crosshairs, as though someone had painted
them on his teeth, and I fired.

"Two," Zlee said, but I knew, and I will tell you that

I never once wondered who those men might be, if they were in love with anyone or if they had families. They were the enemy, and they would stand and fight and try to kill as many men as I might pass in the night to or from the trenches that separated us not just in battle but—we were told—by the will of God, and so I killed as I had been instructed and believed that death and death alone would save me.

Five minutes later, short-range artillery destroyed the kaverne Zlee and I had used for cover, but we were long gone from there and saw the damage only when we walked past on our way to another hide two weeks later.

Weeks. That's how we measured time, a week on patrol there in the mountains surrounding Görz as the winter snows gave way to mud and mist and freezing rain, and a week's rest, during which we rarely did more than maintain equipment, or travel to Ljubljana, where prostitutes, painted and starving, ducked their heads out from alleyways along the river that ran beneath the castle walls, and they begged us for food when they saw that we were only soldiers with no money, which made me feel lonely and then just made me wish we were back on patrol in the mountains, engaged in the careful measure of a not so different kind of hunt.

By April, our commanders wondered where the Italians would attack, not when. Zlee and I were put into service to determine the extent of troop movements, although there was little we could see because of the constantly poor weather that month, mostly rain, and fog from the spring melt, but also the occasional snow squall when the temperatures dipped fast. On one night, the skies cleared enough to reveal a gibbous moon and offer visibility a few miles across the valley, and that's when we discovered deserters going over to the Italians.

There was talk—rumors fed by Slav nationalists—
that the English and Americans were going to help the
Czechs and Slovaks set up a sovereign state, if Austria
and Hungary could be defeated. With the fall of Görz and
the attrition of soldiers, supplies, and ammunition at the
front, it appeared as though the days of the empire's army
really were numbered. For us, though, we were still soldiers of the emperor, and desertion was treason, punish-
able by death.

"Cleansing," Major Márai called it. On the last day
before we were to march down to a reserve billet, we
were called into the company captain's tent and told that
our rest had been canceled. Since we had discovered and
reported the desertions, Major Márai had ordered that
we perform a cleansing in case any other soldiers were
tempted to desert, as well.

"Why didn't you kill the men when you saw them?"
that captain asked us.

Zlee remarked that we had only been spotting, and
by the time we were in a position to fire, the targets had
made it to safe cover.

"You have one of the best kill records of any sharpshooter team at the front," the captain replied. "It's surprising to think that a target might escape you," he added,
as though taunting us. "Pes. That's a Slavic name, isn't it?
Are you a Czech?"

Zlee said he was an orphan, and the captain asked if
he was mocking him. I begged pardon to explain and said
that Zlee had been raised by my father since the two of us
were boys. We spoke Slovak and Hungarian equally well,
and the emperor had our full allegiance. Zlee just stood
at attention, silent.

The captain outlined our orders. We were to set up a hide near the suspected company and wait to see if any other men attempted to cross over. A platoon sergeant, two privates, and a sapper were to accompany us, in order to send up flares and verify any kills, if necessary. I heard Zlee draw breath and waited for him to object to our being sent out with a raiding party in tow, which the captain seemed to expect as well, but Zlee said nothing.

The next night we set our trap, removing guards from that sector under the pretense of a night raid in another. The sergeant who came with us talked too much and kept saying that he could shoot as well as any sharpshooter, and he stomped along behind us over the rocks and fallen trees like an oafish boy in clodhoppers. Then he stopped and lit a cigarette, and Zlee turned and grabbed it from his mouth and crushed it on the ground. The sergeant became furious and shouted at Zlee in the strange stillness of that night, "You are under my command, Corporal Pes!"

"You are under my protection, Herr Stern," Zlee said. "And I can make a bullet in your head look like it came from the enemy, although I might not have to."

The sergeant turned to his infantrymen for support, but they were blank. He spat, cursed his disapproval, and the six of us set off again.

Word must have gotten out, because no one or thing showed itself that night, or the next. In the half-light of the early morning of the third day, a scrawny buck leapt over the ground in front of us and the sergeant ordered, "Flare!"

Zlee was the shooter that hour, but he never lifted the rifle from where it rested on his thigh. The sapper fired on command and the flare riffed in a wavering arc into the faint sky and exploded over the ground before us, bathing that entire section of forested battlefield in green light. The deer stood frozen, dived forward, tripped over its front hooves, regained its balance, and sprinted down the mountain toward the Italians as the flare sputtered and dropped. We got our week's rest after four nights, and when we returned to the line, we hiked through that sector as though it were a worn path or a place forgotten.

WHEN WE WERE WELL OUT OF EARSHOT OF THE SENTRIES, though, we doubled back and took position on an outcropping of rock no more than one hundred yards above where we had sat in a trench with that loudmouthed sergeant and his skittish men two weeks prior. The weather was better, but the moon had waned to new since then, which meant anyone else going out was as blind as we were, until first light, and there we waited.

Sometime just before dawn broke, we heard sentries rustling and whispering, convinced, I suppose, that everyone at war was asleep but them. Then we watched two soldiers, rifleless and shorn of all uniform decorations, go over the top. Though trying hard to move quickly, they seemed to hop in slow motion among the shattered trunks and shell holes that defined the ground.

During our rest, Zlee and I had removed the bullets from one of our clips and reversed the heads. It was something Bücher had taught us. With the flatter back end of the slug at the front of the projectile, the bullet mashes and tumbles as soon as it hits. The Germans used these to penetrate firing plates, and we figured we'd be shooting at moving targets and so would have to aim for the body, which meant that even if the shot hit wide, it would still tear up the chest cavity and be lethal.

I was shooter when the deserters emerged, and I got the first one in my sights, waited as he loped and tucked, and then led him to the right, exactly where he was supposed to step, and shot him between the shoulder blades. When he went down, the other one stopped and looked back. I could see his face as though I were looking through a mirror: young, filthy from not having washed in a long time, eyes big with fear. I aimed for his head, but in that split second I realized that he wouldn't stand in profile like that for long, and so I lowered the rifle as he spun back around, and fired. His arm seemed to whip out from the force of the turn and, when the bullet hit his shoulder, tore off his body and into the air. He dropped and screamed for one involuntary second, then lay motionless and quiet on the ground.

Light was barely discernible, a brief, shadowy dawn particular to the mountains. Zlee glassed the ground and said, "He's still alive."

I could hear the weak sounds of leaves and sticks crackling slowly, and said, "Let's go." He would bleed to death eventually, and there would be short-range artillery soon.

But Zlee said, "They'd have opened up by now. No one over there knows what's going on. We have to finish this."

So we left cover and moved out along a sap that barely came to shoulder height. I didn't like being out in the open so close to morning. The Italians had snipers, too, and I was afraid Zlee was wrong, that someone over there was watching us, but we came to a place where the trench dead-ended against a tussle of roots and rocks, and we settled into that for a hide.

The near-quiet woods and the knowledge that I had

failed to get my kill unnerved and fatigued me, so I handed
Zlee the rifle. He took his time observing the wounded man.
Two minutes, ten—I don't know. His trigger finger moved
slightly along the inside of the grasping groove like it was
stroking a chin, and I whispered, "One hundred and fifty
yards," and noted a fluky breeze. Zlee adjusted slightly for
it, then lay still and breathed slowly as he peered through the
scope, and all I could think about was the light and what a
shame it would be to get killed on a morning as beautiful as
this one. Then Zlee drew the rifle in tight and fired.

From there, we continued north. The line broke and
we bouldered over an exposed but high escarpment above
the Soča, still running, so deep and strangely blue. High
pressure along with the wind seemed to have settled over
the entire valley, and I remembered that it was May. We
came into a new sector just south of Plava and ranged
among the mountains the Italians called the Three Saints,
and which our armies held: Santo, San Gabriele, and San
Daniele. That evening, a Croatian outfit shared with us
their supper of pine-needle tea and gamey horse meat, and
then paraded around two Italian deserters, whom they
were going to shoot in the morning.

"You cold bastards shouldn't get to have all the
fun," they said, laughing and a little drunk on wine
they had found in the basement of an old church. We
kept to ourselves after that and hiked and spotted from
higher ground at intervals that suited us.

One night we camped near a small stream at the back
of San Daniele so that our fire wouldn't be detected.
Artillery thumped slow but steady in the distance like the
ouff of waves on a shore, and Zlee and I ate vodiči we
picked in those hills and boiled with our tea and talked
about Pastvina, my father, and what we hoped to do after

the war. I said that I wanted to travel to America, live by
a pond in Massachusetts, and leave behind everything
about Pastvina, and Hungary, and the people I had no
love for anymore.

Zlee laughed. "Well then, my brother, I'll miss you,
because I'd be happy doing nothing more than living the
rest of my life as a shepherd," he said, with only my
father around to talk to, and that's all he wanted to do
now.

And I thought of the way in which my father had
taken Zlee and shaped him and given him a life he certainly would never have known if he had remained on the
streets of Eperjes with his mother until it came time for
him to go off to war, and I asked him if he had ever heard
from his mother, if he knew where she was, or ever
thought of going to find her.

His mood darkened, and I saw a flash of the old mad
dog in his eyes.

"Find her?" he said. "For years she knew where to
find me, but after a few months of writing to tell me that
she was getting herself back on her feet, and that she had
met a wonderful man who was quite rich and looking forward to meeting me, it all stopped, and your father took
me into the mountains. You don't know how angry those
letters made me, or how many times that winter I nearly
left to go in search of her, just to see her, to see if she had
lied about her life or not. At the camp that spring, I wanted to walk down into the city and find her, and show her
that, in spite of her having left me, I had become a man. I
had even risen early one morning, intent on going, but
when I walked out the door of the cabin, I stood looking
out over the hills. There was a faint light in the sky, a few
sheep bleating, and Sawatch came up and lay down at my

feet. I felt as though I couldn't move, and I thought, What of her rich men and good life? *Otec* and you treat me like a son and a brother, and that's already more than I ever expected to be given in any life."

And that night she came to me in my dreams again, my own mother, and she seemed as fearful as she had been the last time, although she still appeared to be shimmering, as though the beatific perfection of that faded print my father kept, every curve and shadow of which I had memorized as a boy. She waved to me and began to walk away, and I shouted, "No!" She turned and, hands outstretched, said, "Stay, Jozef. You'll be safe," and I begged her to come back, but she kept walking, with her back to me, until she dissipated like a mist.

THREE DAYS LATER, WE CIRCLED BACK TOWARD DIVISIONAL headquarters near Görz and reported in. What we brought the major (we had to bring him something) was news of recently fortified Italian camps, accompanied by troop movement along the entire western stretch of river, from the Bainsizza Plateau down to Görz. Battle was imminent, and the Italians looked determined to make it their last.

It wasn't their last, though. The Austrians expected a spring offensive, and our scouting confirmed this, but the high command's best guess was that the Italians would proceed more tactically than they had in the past, using diversionary incursions upstream to draw our divisions holding the three mountains away from higher ground, and then attacking with their seemingly endless supply of troops. But the Italians had learned nothing in two years of fighting, and the emperor's generals learned that for all of its ethnic factions, diversities, and desertions, theirs was an army of men who would go to their deaths throwing stones at the Italians rather than give an inch of homeland.

And so it began with little more warning than the suspicious activity Zlee and I and a few spotters reported to our command. At first light on the twelfth of May, we had just come off a week's rest and were sitting in a good hide forward of our main trench, from which we had seen an artillery team in range. We wondered why they had exposed themselves so foolishly, but we never thought to question our luck. The officer was easy to identify as his gunners loaded and aimed their cannon. I reckoned him at 550 yards, a long shot, but Zlee never second-guessed himself, or me. Windage was light and the morning air dry, and Zlee just brushed the trigger and I watched that man's head snap back and body crumble as though it had been relieved of its bones.

And hell followed. Three thousand guns—long-range, medium-range, trench mortars, everything—opened fire on us and every other Austrian position from Plava to the Adriatic for two days straight, so that no one or no thing could run, move, or even breathe, a hell in which I prayed to God that I might die so that the banishment toward it would end as quickly as it had begun.

They say the earth is a soldier's mother when the shells begin to fall, and she is, at first, your instinct not to run, but to dig and hold and hug as much of that earth as you possibly can, down, down, down into the dirt, with your fingertips, hands, arms, chest, thighs, and feet, until you are like a child clinging with his entire body to comfort after a nightmare.

But minutes of this, then hours, and days, and you wonder, How many days? Because the earth herself can't stop shaking and disintegrating as the shrieks and howls rain in like otherworldly miscreations on wing who know —*know*—where you are hiding and want not just to kill but to annihilate you, their hissing and infuriate ruts as they approach the last sound you'll ever hear.

In that initial wave, our forward position saved our lives. Lines flanking us to the right and left took hit after hit and the longer-range guns seemed to be inching ahead with each bombardment, stalking our counterbattery fire, command posts, and supply dugouts, so that any response or counterattacks would have to struggle to follow. Yet the Italians seemed interested not in accuracy but fury, and Zlee and I pressed down beneath the cover of canvas we'd used for camouflage and a wall of sandbags we pushed up to take shrapnel for four hours of nonstop shelling, some explosions so close I could feel air being sucked from my lungs.

At what we guessed was late morning, there was a lull. We took our chances and threaded through the warren of dugouts, ledges, and trenches that made up our forward line, the men still in positions that hadn't been completely destroyed looking like gray mannequins in a desolate uniform shop, some doe-eyed and terrified, others appearing resigned to their deaths already. The sergeant who had gone out with us to shoot deserters got hauled past on a stretcher by two bearers, his mouth opened in a scream we couldn't hear (for the bombardment had rendered us deaf) and his chest laid open so clean, I could see his heart beating wildly beneath the bones of his rib cage. The captain's dugout had taken a direct hit. Nothing and no one there by the time we reached it but a horse on its haunches pawing the dirt, and the coppery stink of blood and burned flesh all around.

By noon, the Italians were at full force again, and we had made it to Major Márai's tent just beyond the reserves. He said he wanted us to stay out of the lines and head back to Mount Santo, where they suspected the Italians would attack in strength when the artillery barrage was finished. We were to take any shots we had on high-value targets—officers, cannoneers, scouts.

After a day's hike with a separate regiment, Zlee and I took position on the upper reach of Mount Santo in the ruins of an old monastery's gatehouse, long since reduced to rubble by artillery. The night before, we had eaten field rations of biscuits and hard tack with the same Croats who had fed us when we were ranging from those hills. And at dawn on the fourteenth, the Italians came over the top.

The brigade sent to retake that mountain knew the mixed terrain on the western slope and had been hiding its regiments among the massive stones and stands of trees under the ongoing cover of artillery fire, so that the soldiers defending the mountain were caught off guard, weakened and shell-shocked as they were, as wave after wave of Italian fanti burst from their positions like water from an earthen dam and charged up the steep and bald slopes of those hills, only to be mown down by our Schwarzloses and close-range guns. By late morning, men barely seemed to touch the ground as they entered battle and died in one seamless move, so thickly strewn with bodies were those hills. The few that pushed on toward a trench or rock dugout were shot in the face with pistols, gutted with bayonets, or fought hand to hand, bravery and folly indistinguishable on both sides, until the Italians seemed a being that grew with death and for that reason was incapable of dying, and all we could do was follow our own who had survived and retreat down the steep back of Santo, so that by evening it was in enemy hands.

So holy was it considered, though, that a Czech major general named Novak ordered those same Croat defenders to return the fight on that mountain just when the Italians were at their most vulnerable—in victory. The counterattack was swift and surprising, early in the morning of the next day. From the close-quartered position of the mouth of a collapsed kaverne, Zlee and I watched as the wearied but confident Italians rose from their sleep to the din, stumbled and rubbed their eyes, and there they died in a chaos of bizarre yelps and war cries from the mouths and bellies of men bent on vengeance, and seemingly astonished to find themselves alive.

THE WHOLE OF SUMMER, BATTLE RAGED, THE BLOODY STALE-mate of attack and counterattack proving ineffective for all but the winnowing of souls, so that I came to believe that our stand there on the Soča could not survive, and I wondered more darkly in the back of my mind if we—our empire, our army, the land on which my father had taught me, too, how to survive—had been abandoned by the emperor's God for some sin long forgotten or even unknown to those of us sent to atone for it, an atonement Zlee and I were yet kept from by the simple fact that we were a more useful tool kept alive, though all it would take was for one of us to be hit by a shell, or brought down by something as simple as dysentery, and the other would be useless and so sacrificed.

And no doubt we would have been ordered in the end to stand and die there on the slopes of those mountains, along with half a million other men I'd slipped past silently in a trench or shared tea with in the Austrian Landwehr

when the Italians launched their eleventh battle on the
southern front at the end of that summer had we not been
ordered north to Kobarid with a new regiment of Austrian
Sturmtruppen, without knowing or even questioning why.

The Tolmin bridgehead was only a day behind us
when the Italians let loose from their positions and
fought to cross the Soča, holding their lines this time. In
its first two days alone, the August shelling exceeded the
onslaught we had faced in May and left entire divisions
of men wiped out, save for a few freakish survivors.
Onto the Bainsizza Plateau the Italians charged, resisted
only here and there where air reconnaissance had failed
to identify a well-dug-in company of Austrian riflemen
and machine gunners. And on a day when Emperor Karl
was said to have surveyed the lost battleground from
Čepovan Hill with Borević at his side, the order was
given to retreat from the Bainsizza in order to save what
was left of his loyal army, Borević himself hoping at
least to keep the northern borders of the Austrian
Littoral intact, along with the southern prize of Trieste,
but leaving the Soča south of Luzia to be revered by
Italian soldiers and poets as the Isonzo.

We watched, too, that day, like chosen ones who
turn back to see their city burn, and surveyed the battle
from the northern heights that rose above that river.
None of the men, Austrian or Italian, had faces as they
had when we stood with or against them in battle. It was
the crawl of the fight we witnessed sweeping steadily east
below, the scene broken only by the concentration of
artillery on some holdout sectors, until the mountain
breeze pushed out the cloud of smoke and Italian helmets
continued to poke along the plain and were contested
only intermittently. Then, at our new captain's orders,

we turned away, shouldered our rifles, and hiked in
silence and single file.

IN THE SMALL RIVER TOWN OF KOBARID, TUCKED INTO A
shaded and rugged valley where only a single church with
a rounded bell tower rose above the tiled roofs of the
houses of farmers and merchants who cared little for
whether the rest of the world referred to their home (as
obscure before the autumn of 1917 as some Tasmanian
cove) by a name Slavic or Italian, we ranged among the
Austrian Sturmtruppen with whom we had retreated, and
a number of German forces who had come south from
the western front.

There was no peace or active cease-fire on the river
this far north, but the animus of battle was absent, at
least for the time being, and we returned to the exercise
of watching and ranging, taking the occasional shot at
some poorly disciplined or perhaps new recruit in the
trenches that faced us to the west, but we found that we
were killing less and less, not because our skills were
weakening but because our adversaries were digging in—
whether out of fear or preparation for some engagement
to come, we were unable to tell.

Perhaps, though, they had their scouts, too, who might
have witnessed what we were becoming, old soldiers who
seemed to have marched into a new war. As sharpshooters,
Zlee and I were trained to be invisible and silent. But
for rounds of ammunition, field rations, and water, we
stripped away or left in reserve what the standard infantry
soldier needed—and wanted—in his pack to survive, so
that we could move in and out of hides like jewel thieves.

But the Sturmtruppen of the Armeeoberkomando

carried with them what seemed like the crucial elements of an entire supply truck on their belts and backs—double rations of food, water, gas masks, filters, hand grenades, flashlights, spades, pickaxes, wire cutters, medical kits, compasses, whistles, trench daggers, bayonets, pistols, carbines, and on and on—and still they moved as though every limb of every man followed the orchestrated touches of an overlord, all-seeing, all-knowing, indefatigable, and swift. They drilled in separate units, and although their uniforms never matched a single shade of Austrian gray, their steps did, so that from the distance that Zlee and I often observed them, they appeared a flock of disparate-feathered doves who nevertheless clung in flight to a formation that bolted forward in an instant, left or right, without a single frayed or lagging edge.

The men of our own army were like ambitious recruits compared to the German soldiers who swelled not just our ranks but our morale, men the likes of which we had never seen, soldier paragons who looked as though they could—and would—rise and do battle at a moment's notice, even from the deepest reaches of sleep. They were distinguishable only by the visorless Feldmütze they wore and their indifference to all but the dutiful carrying out of orders, as though they were the very laws of cause and effect. And yet, in reserve, where we maintained rifles and listened to flat-toned stories of days on the Somme (where they said a man was lucky if he could say he had kept himself alive for an hour, let alone the length of a day), they were humorous and good-souled men who laughed at our German (which marked us as Slavs), shared their food and drink equally, never quarreled, and showed respect to anyone who moved with the same command-abiding precision with which they moved.

The world and the war—life and death—were that simple.

When Zlee and I first arrived at the southern front in those spring months that lengthened to feel like years, and ran afoul of Austrian line officers who were convinced that their place above subordinates was given to them by the divine right of kings, we cultivated our own aloofness as sharpshooters to avoid the whimsical orders that issued from those men when they felt the need to be obeyed. But among the Austrian and German troops we fell in with that autumn in Kobarid, we felt the camaraderie of skill and demeanor, and so began to believe again in the possibility of victory in that war, after having lost so many battles, a victory, we would soon find out, that was being mapped out in the mountains above the plateau the generals had conceded to their enemy in order to save themselves and their imperial army.

Gradually it became clear to our high command that the strength of the Italians on the Bainsizza Plateau came at the expense of troops left to defend their lines to the north. This, and the rumors swirling that General Cadorna had no intention of waging war so close to winter, and that even he, their commander in chief, had retreated to quarters in the mountains to write his memoirs. To us, though, what mattered was the martial practice of routine, each soldier to his regiment, and Zlee and I on our own. With permission from our sector captain (after hearing a group of men from the Black Forest say they longed only for something close to the food they had once enjoyed there), we shot a stag in the woods east of our own lines and delivered it up to the mess sergeant, who turned it into a venison stew, which he served with brown bread and beer, items which had showed up mysteriously from Bohemia. There was a feeling of renewed strength

among our company that night, and we rested well, free
from the threat of random artillery and mortar fire, and
woke the next day to a morning cold and clear there on
the river, the air smelling of autumn and cookstoves.

That was a Monday and near the end of October,
which I remember because a priest had come to say Mass
the day before. We knew not a word of his Latin and took
Communion perfunctorily, then stood around wide-eyed
and waiting for the cook to dole out our huntsman's
feast. But before Zlee and I could claim our fair share, we
were summoned to the captain's tent, where we saw again
Sergeant Major Bücher, who had trained us in Klagenfurt.

"*Die Zwillinge,*" he said when we entered, and smiled
his broad smile, his tunic adorned with the ribbon of the
Bavarian Military Service Order. "You have kept well, I see."

We saluted and he took a step toward us with arms
crossed behind his back, as though in the attitude of
inspection.

"We have kept, Herr Bücher," Zlee said, and at this
the man nodded, turned, and lowered his head.

Never, when I set out from Pastvina—all of the world
I knew—did I imagine that war would become such a
lonely and peregrinated life. A soldier lives by nature in
the company of others like him, protecting, trusting, and
much of the pull away from my father and my village was
one born of a desire for common conviction among that
company. We believed in the right of the emperor in those
days, and any man who took up arms believed it to the
end, an end no one feared, for, if it came, it carried purpose and the promise of a kingdom greater even than the
one for which we were willing to fight and die.

And then a skill we honed out of need put Zlee and
me on the path of an isolated, if not a privileged, exis-

tence within that fraying quilt of cultures, tongues, and commanders so at odds and yet capable of taking orders so that men stood and fought and died, and other men took their place, and any notion of camaraderie or company I once had disappeared in the detached deployment of men like us who worked on the periphery of rank and regimental assignment in what they called a modern war, but which bore our mortality along like any other.

None of this I questioned as we moved from place to place, often only hours before destruction rained down upon whoever or whatever remained there, and Zlee and I kept marching forward, believing that this was our fate and no man or weapon could touch us. Until I saw our old mentor that day.

I was glad to lay eyes on Bücher again and probably stood ever so slightly taller in that tent as a result, but I wondered, too (like a child who is playing with a difficult puzzle and to whom the position of a long-passed-over piece suddenly becomes clear), if there wasn't simply a human hand in what I had attributed to some divine purpose, someone, not something, directing us like a general moving an army on a map, though our mover wore an overcoat and a wooden leg and we were the only two pieces he pushed on that map, and I had a bad feeling about where it was Sergeant Bücher was about to send us.

He paced back and forth a few steps and then said to our captain in German, "Attach them to Klammer's regiment. Though Prosch, the bastard, doesn't deserve them."

To us, he said that, while we had trained hard with these men for the offensive that was imminent, he had a request from the Austrian high command for a team of sharpshooters to report to Fort Cherle in the high moun-

tains near Lake Garda, where an Italian sniper had been
taking his toll on the men there.

"It will be a long and difficult passage," he said, "and
the war may even be over before you get there, but this is
what I trained you to do. To hunt and to kill what you
are hunting. Not storm bridges." He snapped to attention, dismissed us, and said, "Godspeed, my friends."

Two days later, in a cold and shrouding mist, while
German and Austrian special forces smashed through
the unsuspecting Italian lines at Kobarid and com-
menced an attack that collapsed Cadorna's army and
forced it to retreat as far as the shores of the Piave
River, Zlee and I hiked north and west into the
Karnische Alpen and jagged Dolomiten, peaks and valleys already covered in wet and deep snows that forced
the unit of Tiroler Landesschützen with whom we traveled onto skis and snowshoes as we crossed the northern littoral, away from the rivers of Italy, and back into
the mountains.

THE NORTHWESTERN CARPATHIANS, IN WHICH I WAS RAISED,
were a hard place, as unforgiving as the people who lived
there, but the Alpine landscape into which Zlee and I
were sent that early winter seemed a glimpse of what the
surface of the earth looked and felt and acted like when
there were no maps or borders, no rifles or artillery, no
men or wars to claim possession of land, and snow and
rock alone parried in a match of millennial slowness so
that time meant nothing, and death meant nothing, for
what life there was gave in to the forces of nature surrounding and accepted its fate to play what role was
handed down in the sidereal march of seasons capable of

crushing in an instant what armies might—millennia later—be foolish enough to assemble on it heights.

And yet there we were, ordered to march ourselves, for God, not nature, was with us now, and God would deliver us, in this world and the next, when the time came for that.

In Tolmezzo, we picked up another unit of Landes-schützen, along with a Bergführer, and separated so that each team would be no more and no less than a day apart, ours leaving one day later. We hiked through the Wolayer Pass to Kötschach-Mauthen (the names of places told to us by our mountain guide), and roads gave way to footpaths, and footpaths disappeared into forests, and what towns and hamlets we came to and passed through, then, didn't matter enough to name, so we hiked in silence, as the soldiers with whom we trekked were inclined.

And they—these soldiers of the east Tirol—bore the years of their own detached fighting in the distinct terrain of the high Alpine war. When we stopped to rest and take water and food, and they removed their protective cloth-ing, I saw fingers missing from frostbite, unkempt beards, and deep carved lines radiating from the edge of their eyes and across scabbed and leathery faces. And although we remained silent as we moved, over tea they (who seemed to know who and what we were) would remind us, in a tone strangely hieratic and as though they could see into our disappointment at having been ordered away from the Soča, that this, too, was a front, these moun-tains borders that separated centuries of their own cul-ture, convictions, and quiet life from the new, false sense of nation that the Italians in their folly had already suc-cumbed to, and of this we had no doubt as we fell back into formation and followed our guides along some path that remained invisible to us and yet to them had been carved in stone by great-great-grandfathers long ago.

As the days wore on, the cold slowed us more than the snow, and had we not the shelter of a mountain refuge each night along the way, we might have survived one bivouac in that terrain but perished by the morning, so fast and hard would those temperatures change, bringing blizzards that kept us snowbound sometimes for days, and the journey that should have taken a few weeks by foot looked more likely to stretch into months.

But even these periods of rest were seen as necessary to the nature of the landscape, and never did I sense any form of boredom or acedia entering into the disposition of those men, so Roman and stoic in the makeup of body and soul were they. When the front that had brought weather cleared out, we rose and pushed on as ordered.

There was nothing to gain by kindness in that war, but those men drew us into their numbers and gave to us from their own store the woolen socks and balaclavas and mittens made of rabbit skin that they wore as we hiked and waited, hiked and waited, week after week, the landscape breathtaking, the altitude increasingly punishing, and we followed the arc of the range south by southwest and into the Dolomiten, where we replaced our alpenstocks with ice axes and strapped nailed soles to our boots and roped ourselves together as we climbed, with Zlee and me in the middle of the team so that the veteran guides could both lead in front and bring up the rear, the paths we walked now discernible only to those guides. And for a few late-autumn days, during which we hiked steadily and without rest until we came to the mountain-top refuges along our way and slept, I felt a sense of peace in that war, within myself, and without, amid the unexpected beauty of those peaks that lured and threatened us like enemies themselves, though a threat unlike the arbitrariness of battle on the Soča, because the mountains seemed in equal measure exacting and prepared to forgive.

Even so, we were reminded of how indiscriminate and cold this enemy who would survive us all was as we approached Mount Marmolada and proceeded up the face, a full traverse the only option we were given. A father and his son, who had joined the Landesschützen together and who knew the mountains so well that they could point out critical discrepancies in the maps issued from the high command, were the last two on our rope and saw too late the thin ice layer that masked the crevasse over which we had all passed, blinded and hunched by exhaustion and the weight of our packs, and the old man dropped through like a stone, pulling the line taut in an instant and his son in a rapid slide toward him, so that the boy (I say this remembering that I was just eighteen at the time, but this lad, strong as he was, could not have been a day over fifteen) had to lean back and dig his heels into the snow as he yelled *"Absturz!"* to Zlee and me, and we dropped and dug in hard with our axes. But the shock and dizziness weakened his footing and he began to slip as the crumbling layer through which his father had broken cracked and shattered and the rope moved through it like wire through wax, so that he, too, now fell as the top gave way beneath him.

Slowly, the weight of two men dangling from that rope began dragging Zlee and me to the edge of the crevasse, until I could peer down into its faint blue and see the boy struggling to right himself in near daylight, while the old man twisted on the darkened bitter end. As we tried to haul them out of that grave, the rope began to slice and fray against the hard crust, our own footing gradually giving way, and I saw the boy look down at his father (whose figure had stopped spinning) and up again at me, then pull his knife out of its sheath, cut the rope above his head, and disappear into the ice.

We continued on, over less daunting peaks, but with the storms and the weather becoming more severe, until one day we forded steep falls, which we were told were the headwaters of the Adige, and in what little talk there was among these men, there was mention of Advent soon, and at the next refuge a makeshift wreath of fresh spruce and paraffin candles unburned and waiting sat on the table, left by villagers or the unit of Landesschützen that had been here before us (although days or weeks before, we weren't sure), and yet there was little else to mark the time since we had left Kötschach and begun our long descent toward the Asiago Plateau, so unremitting was our trek of ascents and descents through the seemingly endless and impassable world of forest, rock, and snow.

And on the last day of November, at an outpost where our team caught up with the unit we had been dogging, Commander Klammer passed around a clear glass bottle of grappa to celebrate his patron, Saint Andrew, and I remembered celebrating the same, my father's name day, each year in Pastvina, the mutton, the rich red Hungarian wine (before he took to slivovica, and the only time drink was ever allowed), the reminder that the old man painted with a parted beard and a scroll brought wisdom and the Word, and this all foreshadowing the Savior the pious men surrounding me said was to come.

My father, who was drunk on so little in those days, used to say with a cherubic smile, although his tone had sounded sad, "There is God in all of this," and I wondered that night in the mountains of Austria if he was right, or if he was bending to the fear that over the years had begun to encompass him, and I said out loud, "Where is God in all of this, Father? Where?" But he was silent there. No word. No wisdom. Was he where I had left him, his kiss dry, his eyes wet? Or was he silent now because he had gone from me? Zlee and I downed our toast of the strong drink that tasted like grapes soaked in turpentine and butter, heard someone who had just been told why it was we were on that odyssey whisper, "*Armer Kerl*," slept fitfully for the cold, and woke before the sun was up to leave with this new unit of Landesschützen, the one that would take us, finally, to Fort Cherle, although, as it turned out, the storm of the winter was yet to descend, and it would be nearly another month of hiking and waiting in the high mountains before we arrived at that garrison.

I REMEMBER STILL, AS WE APPROACHED FORT CHERLE, THE new snow falling on the already deep pack we skied, and the strange lack of harassing fire from either the Italian or Austrian positions as we pushed up the access road that led to the back of the fort, and in the silence of the forest, I thought of Bücher. He had been right about the time it would take us to get there. Had he been right, too, about the fighting and the war?

We reported to Captain Edmund Prosch, a bored and phlegmatic officer assigned to this stalemated outpost. Or maybe he was happy there, away from battle on the open plains below, where our army now pursued with a thirst to destroy its enemy (it was said), news of which he had certainly received, for there was a tone of anticipated victory at Cherle, and everywhere, for that matter, along the northern front. After he looked us over and told us never to report to a commanding officer without having washed and shaved first, he bent down to his papers.

We waited, undismissed, until he looked up and said, as though this was the first day we had spent in the army—and the conversation with our superior officer had in fact been seamless—"You men will do as I say, and go where I tell you to go," and then informed us that there would be Mass at midnight in the fort's refectory. "Mandatory. You're not Protestants, are you?" he asked as he turned back to the papers he kept riffling through, occasionally adding his signature.

I said that we weren't, and he said, "Good. Let them desert to the English all they want, because I would just as soon shoot them coming at me as running away."

And so we moved along the tunnels of that fort to a dank and makeshift chapel, listened in our weariness and the darkness lit by candlelight to the high Latin of the Christmas liturgy, with which we were wholly unfamiliar, and fell off to sleep afterward on folded blankets and steel racks bolted into crumbling bricks, where the cold emanated from the walls.

Fort Cherle stood at the edge of Austrian territory in the high mountains northeast of Lake Garda and straddled the northern Alpine front. From its barricades and walls, its guns traded defensive fire with Italian posts at Campomolon, although it seemed like hubris to believe that these positions had reach enough to claim or even prove that they defined lines and borders in those mountains. All of its firepower was trained forward and to the south, and we were told by a gunnery captain that its roof could withstand sustained direct hits of artillery and that its walls (belowground and encircled by a kind of dry moat) were meant to absorb the impact of shells. Outside, though, a soldier on lookout was in greater danger of being wounded or killed by the limestone shards that a well-placed shell could produce than he was by an army climbing out of the surrounding valley and storming its ramparts.

And as though to dramatize the senseless and unsuspecting terror of the place for us, in the first week of the new year, the Italians began a steady barrage from their 149-mm cannons, enough to make one wonder if perhaps they hadn't chosen this fort as the one place where they would wage an unlikely assault. The rounds were steady and frequent and their accuracy was gaining. Zlee and I were called up to a gunner's post to assess what the fire might presage, and as we climbed into one of the mounts, a near-direct hit slammed into the wall of the moat that surrounded the fort. When we lifted our heads and shook off the dirt, we turned to the two gunners who were manning the M9. Like twins themselves attached to that gun in life and death, they sat unblinking and in disbelief on the iron grillwork of the steps, an ort of sharp limestone in the neck of each, blood pumping out and pouring into their uniforms at the chest every time they gasped for breath, until, in what was perhaps only a few seconds, they took their last. That fort was the remnant of wars no country would ever see again, and I quickly came to despise it, even before I knew what awaited when it came time for me to climb down off of that mountain with the will to fight for the only hope left: to see my father again.

IN MID-JANUARY—IT WAS 1918, THE LAST YEAR OF THE WAR— Zlee and I saw for the first time the work of our adversary. At first, Prosch and his men believed it was random fire and Italian luck that was taking a slow toll on the men who stood lookout at dawn, or who didn't come back from the early-morning hunting party in search of goat. But once they saw that luck had nothing to do with placing a bullet in the head of a man in the same spot every time, they realized they were being hunted by a sniper. The only thing random about him was the frequency with which he killed, this only adding to the cost of morale at the fort, as well as men on lookout. There *was* no frequency, at least any that they could discern. Three days, one week, a month would go by, and then two kills two days in a row, followed by another lull. No pattern emerged, and no artillery seemed able to deter him, or them.

Prosch was the son of a Viennese colonel and he insisted that he be sent his own sharpshooter to hunt for the sniper. A small party of four Landesschützen had showed up in September. They'd gone out, and only one had come back, pale with the loss of blood and dehydrated and able to give up no information on the others, or the sniper, before he died. Two Austrian sharpshooters had been sent in October, just before the advance at Kobarid, and they had been found dead in a cave less than a mile above Cherle, the shooter appearing asleep over the sights of his rifle, the spotter killed with a bullet to the head. Prosch had sent an outraged cable to Ljubljana, and within days, Zlee and I were trudging through those mountain passes because Bücher had become well known and respected at the Austrian high command.

After the harassing fire of New Year's, we wondered, but never questioned, why Prosch kept putting us on lookout just before dusk, when, on that morning in mid-January,

one of the two men who had replaced us dropped with a
bullet through his neck. Artillery responded in the direction of Campomolon, but no one had gotten a good fix
on the shooter's position because the morning was over-
cast and the air had a slight mist to it. Prosch ordered us
to his office and told us to get what we needed from his
lieutenant and "find that son of a whore, or pray that he
finds you first."

From the lieutenant and a bespectacled man in supply
we got beeswax for our boots, a ration of biscuits, an
extra canteen for water, and some small candles we used
to melt snow in our cups, and then we stayed put at the
fort. The temperatures had dipped well below freezing by
nightfall and a sickle moon hung in the western sky, the
air so crisp that it seemed to crackle when you inhaled.
The next day we rose and ranged to the peak of Mount
Cornetto, the best vantage point in the region of the surrounding territory, and safely to the north, but we only
did this to escape the damp cells and crushing morale of
the fort. In truth, we had no idea how we should go about
finding the man or men who most likely thought and
acted as we did, and we even wondered each time we
stepped off of the access road to the fort and into the pine
and rock ledges of the forest, if we'd emerge onto some
height, glass our line of sight, and be killed right where
we stood. But we changed our route every day, found several vantage points and possible hides, overnighted below
the tree line each night in a hidden snow cave we carpeted
with pine needles, and, after a week of this, reported back
to Fort Cherle.

Prosch seemed surprised to see us, or at least he
feigned surprise, and wanted to know why we weren't
out hunting our sniper, as we'd been ordered.

"Herr Hauptman, because he's not out there," Zlee said.

"How can you be so sure?" Prosch replied.

"It's too cold, sir. So we're ranging to find the most likely place for him to reappear when the weather breaks, and for us to position ourselves."

"Splendid," Prosch said. "I've been sent mountain men who have found it too cold to hunt in the mountains. Corporals Pes and Vinich, if one more man dies at the hand of this Italian while you are under my command, there will be no courts-martial. I will execute you both myself and have the stable boys pitch your bodies over a cliff. Do you understand?"

For the first time, I feared what a man was capable of doing to me in that war, a man weaker than I, and yet one whom I was bound to obey, at least in his presence. At that moment, I would have chosen to have been blown to bits by random artillery rather than to have had Captain Edmund Prosch be the last man to see me alive before a firing squad put a bullet through my heart.

But Zlee never flinched. "Herr Hauptmann, if you will forgive the solitary nature of our methods and allow me to explain."

Zlee's German sounded nothing like the high tone he had meant to use, even if sarcastically, but Prosch, who loved to be coddled almost as much as he loved to be feared, sat down and said, "Explain."

And so Zlee told him that we suspected the sniper had been using the intermittent warming trends in the mountains to hunt in the early mornings, when the mist that rose from the melting snow provided a kind of directional cover for him, while it still allowed him to fire accurately using an optical sight, because the scope picked up more morning light than the naked eye. And in the thin mountain air, the closer he got to his target, the more accurate he'd be.

"He's not firing from the next mountain over, sir," Zlee said, "but more likely only a few hills." We couldn't know this for sure, but it was our best guess, and so we told Prosch something he wanted to hear.

Prosch asked why the other Austrian sharpshooters hadn't known this and Zlee said that unfortunately they had overestimated the skill of their adversary. "If he were good at what he does, sir, he would be wearing a coat of field gray and fighting for Emperor Karl." Although we ourselves suspected our target to be a local Austrian trained like us, yet who, for reasons only he knew, had switched sides.

Zlee then explained that we would do nothing until a warm front came through, in anticipation of which we would set out in the direction of the peak to the north of us, settle into our hide, and wait for the shooter to show himself.

"How do you propose to see him before he sees you, or, more likely, kills another one of my sentries?" Prosch asked. The corner of his mouth lifted to what looked like a faint smile every time he posed a question, and I wondered if he was using us and every other sharpshooter who had come through here for a bizarre game of cat and mouse that broke up the boredom of his war.

Zlee said that on the morning when the temperature rose above freezing, the sentry would be a mannequin, "the best likeness your man in supply can create." We would attempt to get a visual on him, and at the very least would see his muzzle flash when he fired. With that, perhaps, we might be the ones to fire next.

Prosch stood, head down, for what seemed like too long, and then he looked up at us. "A ruse. Yes. I like it. Don't worry, Corporal Pes, our sentry will be so lifelike, you'll expect him to salute. All that will remain is for you and your twin to shoot straight, and well."

It was almost a month before the mercury rose above zero in those mountains, an evening in late February, when full cloud cover came in after a day of strong sun and trapped the heat. Already, each week seemed to bring more daylight, and you could feel the moisture rising and evaporating in the air, so we reported to Prosch and had the night sentries replace the man who was to take over at 0400 with our dummy.

They gave him a cigarette at 0600 and had the sentry prop him up so that his face showed through a gun mount on the parapet. That same sentry had orders to lie on the floor next to the mock guard until 0800, or until someone fired in his direction, after which he was to yell as loud as he could, while still undercover, "*Sharfschütze!*" The artillery commander gave the forward gunners orders to wait for three minutes after the shot and then to fire in the direction of Campomolon, regardless of whether they could tell exactly from where the shot had come.

From sunset until first light, Zlee and I watched from a tight grouping of rocks just above the tree line a mountain away, expecting the shooter to be hiding in a slow-rising forest of firs that began at an elevation slightly higher than Cherle, about six hundred yards east-southeast of the fort. If we were right, we'd have a long but clear shot across the valley, a distance of almost eleven hundred yards, we reckoned, the longest we'd ever attempted, longer than any Austrian sharp-shooter had ever recorded, but the closest we could get to this enemy who knew those mountains better than we did without letting him know that we were there, too.

There was a long and deceptive silence then on that battlefield of peaks and crags and valleys, as the sky lightened and the snowcaps reflected changing hues of rose, until, within minutes, as though the curtain had lifted on a play we'd written below, we heard the crack of a rifle and a distant more urgent cry of "*Scharfschütze!*" and then another crack, soon after which (too soon by my count) artillery let loose a hurried salvo into Italian territory, and everything was quiet again.

Zlee never took the shot. With the rising mist came a breeze, strong enough to make his long-distance attempt no more accurate than if he had been looking down the barrel of a musket. As for me, spotting into that dawn from a distance too great, I could see nothing of what was unfolding down below, and so we were caught not knowing what to do. If we abandoned our hide and reported back to Prosch, we'd be marked ourselves, and not likely to get another chance to outshoot our shooter. If we stayed put, there was no guarantee he would return to the same position for more hunting the next day, or any day after, and Prosch would certainly believe that we had deserted. He'd only be happy only with the head of some foe on a silver platter, a dish we might just be able to deliver, though, if we trusted our instincts, and luck did the rest. What did we have to lose (besides our lives) by staying put for another twenty-four hours and finding our man before he could strike again the next morning?

And yet, it seemed hopeless. "We've had a good run," I said to Zlee. "If he doesn't show in the morning, or the wind is even trickier, we'll pack up and move north, or west. It'll be spring soon, and this war has got to come to an end someday. We wouldn't be the first soldiers to have shed a uniform and disappeared."

His face as blank a slate as ever, Zlee just shook his head, and I didn't know if it was out of disappointment for his own failure or my suggestion that we desert.

"If only for the wind," he said, "if only for the wind. I could see that bastard's shoulders sticking up above those boulders like he'd been trained to shoot at a carnival. Hell, let there be more fog. I could see his muzzle flash. What a shame, Jozef, if we have to end it like this."

We sat in our hide the entire morning, melting snow into a cup of pine needles until we knew that we had waited too long, and there was nothing left for us to do but to stay and hope we'd get one more chance to face our antagonist, for that's how we thought of him now, this actor who opposed and called into question our very selves. In the meantime, we listened for the dogs and the party of soldiers we thought would be sent out to find us, but no one or thing stirred. And when the sun disappeared behind the highest peak, Zlee said out loud and to no one, "Because you are neither hot nor cold, I will spit you out."

High clouds rolled in without precipitation that night and the air warmed. We slept in hour shifts, and, after 0300, spotted in intervals of thirty minutes to keep our eyes sharp. At first light, the clouds began to disperse, and by the time dawn shone, the same stalking mist rose from the snow, although appearing lighter, so that visibility was improved. I glassed the hide from where the shooter had fired the day before, and there he sat, looking like a man in his own library.

Zlee woke up and took a mouthful of water, and then, fully alert, said, "Tell me."

I confirmed the range of eleven hundred yards and noted that windage was zero across the entire distance, and, through the light mist, the target was in our direct line of sight. Zlee nestled into his stance and began to breathe steadily. I continued to observe and watched the target turn in our direction, as though oblivious to us and our purpose, and noted to myself that he was right-handed, so that when he turned back to take aim at someone or something at Fort Cherle, his cheek and face were covered by the gun stock. And yet he looked oddly familiar, until I realized that he was one of the Tiroleans from our sharpshooter school who had been returned to his regiment, and by the time this was clear to me, Zlee had already adjusted his sight for the distance, drawn breath, and said, "Christ forgive me."

And I heard him exhale with a grunt and felt the warm, moist touch of blood on my face, head, and hands, the report echoing a few seconds later in the high mountain air.

I dropped my field glasses and rolled as the next shot shattered the scope on the Mannlicher, but I knew that it was meant for me. It had come from behind, at four o'clock to our position's twelve. We'd been set up between two shooters, and caught in their cross fire with a ruse that made ours pale, and all I could do was keep moving fast and low as I scrambled along the ground and kicked up snow. I moved crabwise around to the front of the stone that shielded us to the south and got into a position that protected me from the shooter behind but left me exposed to the one who had been sniping at Cherle across the mountain. I crawled over the rock and back into our hide, propped Zlee's inert and lifeless bulk against it, and pushed him over the top and down the other side.

I spoke to him as I worked, told him who had hit him, that the useless jokers were pretty good after all but that I'd have him out of there and out of danger soon, so that we could go back to the fort, finish the war, and get home, and I crawled over that rock and out into the open myself and waited for the next shot to hit me.

When it came—from the south this time and the shooter in the valley—I had Zlee over my shoulder just as I was about to drop down an embankment for cover. I felt the force of the bullet as it slammed into his side at the height of my neck and I fell off balance and rolled toward a cliff and tried to grab at the ground with one hand while holding on to Zlee's body with the other, but our weight gathered too much speed and momentum on the incline, and as I approached the sheer edge, I grabbed a scrub pine growing from a crack in a formation of rock and let Zlee's body tumble down into the ravine.

I HUNG ON TO THAT TREE FOR SOME TIME, WONDERING IF I shouldn't let go, let go and remain with my brother, rather than having to trek again through the mountains and snows of a hostile and desolate country, until my arms began to grow tired and that weariness shook me hard, and I found the will and enough strength to swing my legs and mantle my body up onto the ledge. I sat there, willing grief and sorrow as the sun began to bend to the west and I felt a chill, knew that there was no time now for grief, and realized that I had lost my hat and gloves, canteen, field glasses, and rucksack, and could find only my knife still sheathed where I kept it tied to my leg.

In my mind, I climbed with stealth and nothing but a good coat and that knife to the side of the shooter to the north, caught him by surprise, and slit his throat. Then I walked back south to where his twin waited for him, approached from behind the boulders that gave him shelter, whispered "*Boom*," and in the confusion slid into his hide and thrust my knife—still soaked with the blood of his comrade—into his chest. And with two rifles and two days' rations, I hiked north and east—not west but east—back into the Karnische and through the lands of the empire, toward the only home Zlee had said he'd ever known, or wanted to know.

But I knew, too, that both shooters were long gone by now, not certain but convinced, perhaps, that I had been hit and fallen to my death. And so I waited for nightfall and retraced my steps back to Fort Cherle.

There was a full moon, but it was bitter cold. I wove some soft fir branches together to cover my head, and walked (when I could) with my bare hands thrust into my armpits. I risked being shot by the sentry if they had changed the password, but this seemed a small and ironic threat to me in the new dawn, and at the command "*Halt!*" I replied, "Don't shoot," then gave my name and rank and the password from three days before. There seemed some hesitation on the other side, until the men could see who I was by my uniform, and I was led like a prisoner into the fort.

I stood outside the iron door of Prosch's office long enough to wish I had walked the other way until I could walk no farther, and then I was escorted inside. I was shivering from the cold, and Prosch, in my defeat, let me shiver.

"Our dummy took a bullet in the neck, just as planned, Corporal Vinich," he said. "And when my sentry, the fool, stood to alert the gunners, he took a bullet in the head. Not as planned, Corporal Vinich."

I tried to control my breathing while he paced.

"Corporal Pes?"

I said, "Dead, sir."

"You leave your brother behind I see. And you disobey orders."

I said that our orders were to hunt an enemy sharpshooter, not knowing that there were two. "But they knew," I said. "About us they knew."

Prosch walked slowly out from behind his desk, removed his sidearm—a gleaming German 9—and held it to my forehead. "Speak without being asked a direct question again, Corporal Vinich, and those words will be your last."

We stood motionless and in silence like that as I waited for what he would do next, until Prosch holstered his weapon and turned back to face his wet stone wall.

"Make yourself useful," he said to the wall. "Take two men from the kitchen for a hunting party and go find a deer or a goat or a goddamn mastodon. I don't care. Shoot it and get us some meat. I'll decide what to do with you tomorrow. Dismissed."

I shot a scrawny red deer at dusk that day, and a pregnant doe the next. The men with me hauled them out of the forest and gutted them at the fort, where a thin venison stew was served in the mess hall at every meal, the cook even making use of the tongue and the brains. For a week after, I was on what felt like perpetual guard duty at dawn every morning, Prosch no doubt hoping I'd be the next sentry to take a bullet in the face, until the high command requested that Fort Cherle send a platoon of men to the fort in Luserna and await for further instruction there, and I was stripped of my lance corporal's star, issued an ill-used carbine, and made the forty-first man in

that platoon when we fell in and moved out the following day.

Soldiers rarely get to glimpse the maps of the high
command and they maneuver out of discipline and duty
to those positions where they are ordered, pawns needed
to stand and hold until the enemy is drawn out and
exposed, at the expense of many pawns. Prosch knew
that an Austrian offensive was being planned for June, a
pincer attack similar to what the Germans had helped us
achieve at Kobarid, and that the two points of the fight
would be on the Piave River and in the mountains of the
Trentino, where Fort Cherle would provide supporting
fire and sharpshooters would remain invaluable. But in
the mud trenches of a river plain, there was room for
nothing but cannon fodder, so he handed down my death
sentence, betting that I might kill a few more Italians
before it was my turn for the firing squad of dysentery,
machine guns, and long-range shells.

But I had neither the vision of command nor the
recourse to question an officer, and so I marched east that
spring with the ragged souls of that platoon, led by a lieutenant so green no one seemed to know his name, or even
cared to inquire. At Luserna, we joined two more platoons
and were put under a captain who had never commanded a
company, and sent through the Valsugana along the Brenta
until we came to the upper Piave River, and then marched
south along the line that Austria held precariously.

It was early April when we came to the edge of the
Asiago Plateau and began our descent toward a river
island called Papadopoli, and I glimpsed for the first time
the heights to which I'd climbed into those mountains
when Zlee and I made our approach from the Soča, what
seemed now like years ago. The men of our company had

slogged hard through deep, wet snow and then the impassable mud conditions that came with the spring melt, and
we were hungry and exhausted and believed (there was
scant evidence that our army could push any farther past
this river, or even hold its line defensively) that the mud
plains and beds that continued to widen would become
our graves.

One morning as I looked down at the river flowing
below through a valley already turning into a tapestry of
greens, yellows, and whites as far as the blue of the
Adriatic, and back to the still snowcapped and wind-
blown mountain range behind, rising all at once far into
the Alps, I realized that I had no desire and no drive to
fight anymore, no rage at having been wronged somehow, no belief in the right and purpose of kings. I longed
only to turn back and climb and begin life all over again
in a place where I might find the peace I'd once known
in mountains of another time and another place, and I
wondered—if I could slip out of camp unobserved—
whether I just might be able to stay hidden and uncap-
tured until this war came to an end. But in the same
moment this will to live overtook me, we were ordered
to fall in, and so we shouldered our packs and rifles and
set out like thin sheep kept in line with the promise of
food and sleep, too numb to expect our slaughter. And
we marched no better.

DAYS DRAGGED ON, THE WEATHER WET, COLD, AND UNSETTLED.
What food we had became scarcer and scarcer as we
moved closer to the heart of the army I'd once known
from the hills of Görz, and by the time we reconnoitered
with the regiment to which we'd been assigned, we were

down to two days' ration. As a whole, the regiment fared worse. Stretched, their food (what our company could have eaten in twenty-four hours) would last three days. Fuel for their trucks was long spent, so they walked and moved slowly as a result. And all but two horses had died from disease or exhaustion, a lack the soldiers as well as the officers felt, since horses became meat when they were no longer a good means of transport. The men—among whom I was just another Infanterist, a private, determined to stay alive—turned as gray and thin as the spring snow on the side of the road. Some ate what they found rotting in towns we passed through, or drank deliriously from wells fouled and abandoned. When they couldn't move from their own vomit and diarrhea, we left them with what good water we could spare and moved on.

We arrived at our position on Easter of that year (the sight of a sad and slight old priest dressed in white vestments and setting up for Mass on the altar of a box of ammunition my memory of the day) and camped on the Montello rise, where we had a commanding view of the Italian trenches to the west of the Piave, and I fell ill with a fever that same night. The last conscious things I remember were the purposeful movements of the lieutenant, who still commanded our platoon, to make a comfortable bed for me to lie in while I sweated and shook, and the look of concern on his face as he knelt over me and mopped my forehead with a rag he soaked in a bucket of river water.

We had never exchanged more than passing comment in our entire march south, but he seemed a tempered and rational man, even second-guessing a sergeant's estimate of range in the mountains and—out of nowhere—asking me what I thought, and so I told him that I believed that the target was at least a thousand yards farther than what he'd been offered, to which he nodded his assent, and which turned out to be true. He whispered softly (though with urgency) to me that night and coaxed me to drink a brew of herbs he said, as though speaking to himself (because he thought that I had already lost consciousness and couldn't hear him), that he had bartered from a Hungarian and boiled down, and then told me to sleep while he sang an old Slovak song that I had learned as a boy about a shepherd who has a vision of the Virgin Mary and becomes a great soldier for Christ.

And in my delirium, I dreamed of my mother once again. This time, we were walking together and I was telling her about my life in Pastvina and how I missed my father now that I understood the wisdom I had mistaken for weakness, and that I wished she could have been with us there to watch over him as she had watched over me. She didn't speak, but kept staring with the same bright and shimmering face of the woman who had first come to me as a boy, on the boat from America to the old country.

Then, in the distance, I heard what sounded like a train approaching, the sound of its wheels and engine growing and growing until it was clear that it was coming toward us. Suddenly I couldn't move and she let go of my hand, her face changing to the stern pose she wore in the daguerrotype, although the image of her still clear and distinct in front of me. And she said, "Jozef! Hurry. Come to me!"

But I couldn't move. I was pinned down and felt as though I was being smothered. "Jozef," she was almost yelling now, "you must!"

But as she said this, her image began to fade, even as she implored me more and more to go with her, until her voice trailed off into a beseeching echo, and the oncoming train roared overhead, with nothing in its wake but the dark and a few faint wails like that of a baby, or a lost boy.

I woke, to find the lieutenant standing in the trench with his back to me and looking out over the no-man's-land of the river plain. He heard me stir and turned.

"That was a long night, sir," I said, my own voice sounding hollow.

"Night? You were out for three days, Vinich. I had to convince the captain for two of them that you were only exhausted from the march and that you'd be up in no time, and so he turned a blind eye."

He stood and hobbled on one foot for a moment, then placed more weight slowly on the other. I asked him what had happened and he said that on the third day British planes had begun a wave of bombing and strafing runs over our positions. A new unit coming up to the line led them straight to our company, and they went at us all day like hornets from an overturned nest. On their last run, the lieutenant saw the plane that was coming in directly for us. I was huddled in a blanket. He wrapped me tighter and pushed me into the corner of the trench, then threw himself on top of me as the plane opened up with a burst of machine-gun fire. All around him men who couldn't find cover were shot to pieces, those not killed outright screaming from the burning of the wounds the plane's guns inflicted. Another one came in along the same line and dropped a shrapnel bomb as it banked up and away from the trenches and our poor attempts to return fire. The bomb fell just behind of where the lieutenant and I had taken cover, and a piece ripped along the dirt wall and tore into the side of his calf.

"The bleeding stopped this morning," he said, and showed me the muddy bandage he had found to dress the wound. "I've been drinking more of this Gypsy brew than you have. But I'll live to fight."

I must have looked dazed, still, from the fever, but he knew what I was thinking. Just another foot soldier who should have been sent to a field hospital in reserve, from which everyone knew he'd never return, and yet there I was, left to ride out the same fever that had been striking hard up and down the lines. The lieutenant took the gold-colored sharpshooter lanyard I had removed and kept secreted in my breast pocket, and he said, "You don't want to have this on you if you're captured, and with what's coming, I'm going to need someone who can shoot."

His name was Holub, his father a Czech from Vienna and his mother a Slovak from Pozsony. He was in his final year of university, where he studied philology, when he was conscripted and sent to the front in the fall because of the army's desperate need for line officers. He had been cold, hungry, seen men dead and dying, he said, but had never been in battle, and he hoped that he would get the chance to fight the Italians before he died in this damn trench. I was silent the whole time he spoke, grateful to my savior but tired of the war and talk of Austria's superiority, and I hoped, too, for his sake, that Lieutenant Holub would see battle soon and that it would be fierce and unrelenting and that he would die quickly and well.

By May 1918 we were being resupplied with everything from horses and trucks to artillery, bullets, coffee, and plum brandy. Our own air support dropped food—tins of meat and loaves of bread, along with battle rations of hardtack—and officers made sure that men at the front had what they needed to maintain as much morale as one could hope for under the circumstances.

Early June and the last of the troops ordered to the front along the Piave had sneaked beneath their cover of camouflage and taken up position in the alleys of defense we had sculpted out of the stripped and barren mud. Men deserted when they saw squadrons of those British planes take control of the skies, and when they looked to the left and right of them and saw not an army ready to burst from those trenches for a fight, but thinned pockets of sick and dirty men weary from having survived a destruction.

And yet, and yet. Those who rose to stand-to every morning still believed in the genius of Borević and the divine guidance of our emperor. It was that kind of world. The Italians were hated fiercely, and there were still enough veterans of Kobarid around who had watched them turn and flee ("Like rats!" they said, laughing with derision) in the autumn of 1917 to tell their comrades that soon, if they fought "as hard as we fought on the Soča," well-provisioned Italian trenches would be theirs. And then on to Venice and Milan.

"Soldiers!" the generals exhorted us in a message on the eve of battle, "Your fathers, your grandfathers, and your ancestors have fought and conquered the same enemy with the same spirit. You will not fall below them. You will rise above, and overthrow everything before you."

On the morning of the fifteenth of June, our guns began at 0300, throwing across the river at the Italians everything we had left. For two hours, our artillery pounded the far shore and I listened and waited in the ranks with indurate men whose disdain for death had become a filth they let cover themselves and seemed even to display like a talisman, and new recruits who longed to fight instead of starve at home now saw battle for the first time and wept, wet themselves, or tried to run, even after a captain, to make an example, put a bullet through the head of a fresh cadet whose hysterics threatened to unman everyone within earshot of his howls.

We had dug in well with what time, food, and tools were given us. We used riveting of logs, straw, and wire mesh to shore up the banks of mud and stone, so that even though the odd shell or lucky aim dropped directly into our trench works and took its toll of whatever soldier stood his ground there, we underwent the torture of holding hard to our resolve with forbearance, terror, and resignation.

Light came with mist and the smoke of battle, and into it sappers moved like ants to construct pontoon bridges that would let us ford the swollen river. Little more than an hour later, we were given orders to fix bayonets and move out, and I felt a sense of freedom—not fear—as I went over the top and moved onto the floodplain without hesitation, as though my entire being had been let loose by a trigger pull.

The wet ground sucked at our feet, but we struck fast, astounded and buoyed up by the accurate and punishing support our own artillery provided for us in the dawn. At the water's edge, the bridge sections banged and jostled against their fittings as they floated on the thick current, and, still trotting, we bent low to cross them, hoping the anchors at both ends would hold until every man had gone over.

There were other dangers. Our big Škoda guns hadn't managed to take out all of the Italian machine-gun nests, and these strafed the bridges when the first units attempted to pass and killed more than half of our men before trench mortars found the right positions. British planes began coming in waves for more bombing runs, so we held back when we heard the drone of their approaching. And when the stream of men surged again, Italian riflemen plied their trade along the banks. Lieutenant Holub went over the top and onto the bridge with us, and when I saw him stumble as we were midstream, I thought his leg had given out, or that he had been hit, but it was the soldier in front of him who had been shot full in the chest, so that Holub tripped on him as the man dropped and rolled into the water, and we pressed on at the double.

When we reached the other side, we took up position in an abandoned Italian trench. All but one of our platoon had made it across, and we regrouped in order to continue our advance. There was little in front of us, though. The cannoneers had done their work. Limbs and litter were everywhere, the bodies of stretcher bearers lying next to the men they had come to remove, and on the wind the bitter taste of gas mingled with the smell of burning pine. By day's end, we had advanced west, uncontested, into a forested rise, from which we could look back out over the Piave. Some of the dead we had seen wore English uniforms, their Lewis guns (which we had heard about) smashed relics of their firepower nearby, and so we knew that the Italians, who still outnumbered us, had Western support on the ground as well as in the air. It was only a matter of time before we found the place at which they had ceased to retreat and turned to make their stand, and it came to us on the next day with a counterattack in the morning, which by noon we had barely repelled. We had the better position, fortified with several Schwarzloses, and so held our ground with machine-gun and rifle fire against the endless charge of the enemy.

But we lost many men, too. To the north of our position, a group of Italian soldiers penetrated the trench with grenades and fell into hand-to-hand combat until they were killed with knives and pistols. Reinforcements we had expected on the following day never arrived, and we barely held off another counterattack because of the high ground we maintained.

Two days later (it might have been the nineteenth or the twentieth of June, but I had no way of keeping track of days within the month, only the rising and setting of the sun), two new companies made it to our side—part, another new lieutenant among them said, of an entire division of men thrown into the fight by General von Wurm, in the hopes of opening a gap in the Italian lines and pushing through once and for all.

The next day, we stood to with bayonets fixed, and Holub said to me in the trench, as though a veteran of battle, "Stay right beside me," and we went over the top into a wall of Italian machine-gun and rifle fire, the enfilade so close that we were pinned down instantly, and I felt the heat of the rounds, wondered how it was I hadn't been hit and killed, turned to Holub for direction, and saw his body lying next to me, eyes wide open as he stared at the sky, his chest and belly torn apart. Officers in the rear ordered men to advance, and those men were mowed down. When the attack was abandoned, we crawled back into our position and sat numb and indifferent, like prisoners who had just received a stay of execution, until new orders came on the morning of the following day: a full-scale withdrawal back to the east bank of the Piave.

Because we were in one of the forward positions of the advance, our company made up the flank in retreat. Horses, trucks, artillery caissons, and men poured over the Piave under even greater danger from aircraft and machine guns now, because our supporting guns had gone silent from ever more accurate Italian fire and the continuous, lethal presence of British planes. The Italians were hungry for their revenge, now that it was clear that we had nothing, nothing left at all. They weren't going to let an enemy who had humiliated them on their own soil simply walk across the river to lick his wounds. When I took up my defensive position on Papadopoli Island with what was left of our platoon and prepared to retreat the unlikely half mile across the eastern branch of the river to safety, I heard the whistle for an attack come from the Italian side, and so I could do nothing else but take up my weapon to stand and defend the troops retreating.

At eighty yards, the machine guns to the left of me opened up on soldiers moving quickly in a forward advance. The gunners let go in tight, short bursts, aiming for where the men ran bunched up. I drew down on the ones quick enough to break for cover and dropped them with single shots to the waist. Another fellow rifleman to my right—a boy no older than sixteen—fired with a control and accuracy so well trained and deadly that I believed for a moment that it was Zlee at my side and that we'd get out of this alive. But the waves of men coming over those embankments seemed to grow higher and higher. Our defensive artillery, and any commander who might order men to come up and fight, had turned to the logistics of flight and left us to fend for ourselves in this position, which was becoming more sacrificial than defensive, and it was only a matter of time before we ran out of ammunition and were overtaken by the storm.

Upriver, no more than a hundred yards, I saw an enemy unit make it to our barbed wire and begin cutting, and I realized that the division in charge of these positions had chosen ground that left a gap of cover between the machine guns' range and our trenches. I heard a few explosions and their guns stopped. I knew that soon the fight would come down to grenades and knives. I bolted a new round, and as the gunners to my left stopped to reload, they were shot dead in quick succession. I turned and could see a sweep of enemy soldiers attacking from ground that a company of Honvéd had been ordered to hold for the retreat, but they, too, had cut and run.

I pushed the dead men and their gun tripod over and got down in a prone position behind them. My nameless comrade of the trench kept firing at the unit advancing in front of us until more than he could kill with one rifle came at him and he fell back from a bullet in the face, and I was alone, to fight, retreat, or die like those whose bodies lay off to the side as though they were asleep in spite of the din surrounding us.

When I stood to return fire, I saw a new wave of infantry, hushed and spurred, advancing upon the island. Two men with a light machine gun dropped into a shell hole out in front of me, and I waited for the soldier feeding the belt to lift his head to see where I had taken position, and when he did, I shot him and ducked for cover again. Some enemy rifle fire ensued, but I had silenced the machine gunners, or so I thought, when a burst opened up above me, stopped, and then hammered—as though enraged at the delay I had caused them—into the now ripped-up carcasses of the dead men covering me.

I had one more round in my clip, and Zlee's ghost had fallen too far from me to crawl to him for what cartridges might remain in his field pouch, and I knew that the next time I stood would be my last. I thought of my father and wondered what it would be like to live a life as long as his, if I would have become him in the end, weaker but wiser from all that's lost as well as hard-won, and if he might have preferred to have died a young man full of ambition. And I thought of Zlee and what he would do now, surrender or fight to the end, and I wished that we could have sat and talked about the mountains and hills of Pastvina, or at least said good-bye to each other like brothers. I had lost all faith in the belief that I would see those I loved again, but I didn't want to die and disappear like every other soldier who fought and died and decayed in the flood and layers of indifferent rivers and mud. And I was overcome with fear.

I rose and threw my hands up, heard a rifle crack, and spun around as though someone had grabbed my right arm and heaved me. My fingers felt numb, and then as though they were on fire, and as I, too, lay on the ground in our trench among the bodies of all the others, one of the soldiers—an Italian, from the look of his uniform—entered the trench from the side and stood over me with his rifle pointed at my head.

"Please," I said in English.

He fired. Dirt from the ground where the bullet struck beside me sprayed and stung my face.

"*Please*," I begged, not for myself, but for all of the men I had killed because I had been trained never to miss.

He cursed, chambered another round, and raised his

rifle again, when an English soldier ran up from behind him and pushed him away.

"We don't execute prisoners, mate." He scowled at the Italian, yanked me to my feet, and smashed me in the ribs with the butt of his rifle. I doubled over in pain but willed myself not to drop to my feet again.

"Bloody good shooting, you bastard," he said, not knowing that I understood every word. Then he began to search me, even though I was in a position no sharp-shooter would ever have considered a hide, or even been given an order to take up, as he looked for patches, field glasses, rifle scope, maps, or diagrams I might have made, all signs of a sniper. But all that I'd left back in the moun-tain ravine where Zlee lay dead and frozen, all but the lanyard, which Lieutenant Holub burned in a candle flame on the far side of the river before we made our final attack.

The Italian cursed louder and mock-inspected his rifle, while the Englishman ignored him, pocketed my dagger, and shoved me down the wet and narrow corri-dor of mud and out into a wide-open and clearing sky.

"Get a fucking move on," he said, and I remember that, the accent, the scorn in that soldier's voice, the way in which fighting a war seemed just another thing this man not much older than I had been trained to do well, and so did it, as I had done, for the fighting was over now, and I raised my arms above my head and felt blood as it dripped slowly and soaked into my filthy uniform sleeve, cooled in the air, and rested on my skin.

PRISONERS WHO HADN'T BEEN MAIMED WERE FORCE-marched from the Piave to Varago. Roads were littered with the dead, Austrians killed while running or making a final stand, Italian soldiers yet unclaimed. Some looked as though they were slumped over with sleep and that a shout as we passed might rouse them; others were caught in bizarre attitudes and poses, twisted, spitting, begging. One blackened figure knelt with head down and hands open, as though waiting to receive a blessing. Overhead, tight squadrons of planes buzzed loud and low, and the echoes of artillery still rumbled in the east. Not one of us—hundreds of us—said a word as the Italians barked orders and took whatever chances they could to abuse us. For the first time since becoming a soldier, I despised my enemy, now that I was unarmed and no longer had the desire or the means to kill him.

We marched south by southwest. The clouds lifted and I could tell by the sun in which direction it was we were going. A young Italian patrolling our column (no more than a boy in a uniform that shined for not having been washed yet) hit me in the shoulder with some martial-looking ornamental staff and the pain that shot down my arm to my hand became searing and relentless, so that I halted and tottered and nearly dropped, but the prisoner behind me (a Bosnian, his accent thick and guttural, though I understood him) said to be strong and held me up.

"*Halt den Mund!*" the boy shouted in German, and I stood, took a deep breath, and stepped back into line. Through the filthy puttee that I had taken off my leg and wrapped around my hand, I could feel only my thumb. The rest might just as well have been hacked off and discarded.

We were marched to a concentration camp on the outskirts of a town they called San Biagio di Callalta. The camp was a sorting station for Austrian prisoners of war, and from there we followed the road to Treviso and stopped in another camp near the town of Noale, where they began separating us according to nationality. I found myself among Czechs and Slovaks entirely, in spite of the fact that I answered in German every question I was asked.

In the camps, there was talk of the Czecho-Slovak Legion, an army being mustered to defend the borders of the new country, and men who bore the lynx-eyed features of the Slavs saw to it that we had a bath, bread, meat, fresh drinking water, and a tarpaulin to sleep under. It was hard to believe, until, in the morning, they offered every one of us a gun and freedom from Italian prison if we agreed to put on another uniform and fight to protect our nation from a weakened but vengeful Hungary. "Those same princes who had deserted us in battle when we needed them most," they said, men who (I suspected) had never seen battle.

What was a Czecho-Slovak to me, though, a boy raised among Carpathian peasants in a Magyar culture, professing loyalty in a poor school to a Habsburg, and speaking a language in secret they spoke in a land called America? What could those Czech propagandists tell me about nationality? Yet, on and on they went, the Bohemian officers of the legionnaires, telling us that the Hungarian king had kept us in his pocket for centuries, that our own nation was a right to us, and that a Czecho-Slovak division was already being trained to fight against the Austrians in the mountains.

"We are giving you the chance to fight now for yourselves!" they said with a flourish that seemed more bombastic than persuasive.

I said no, and didn't say that I had hunted and put bullets through more than one man who wanted to desert, Czech or Slovak, Austrian or Hungarian. It didn't matter. I had killed enough for several countries and was happy to stay in prison, where I belonged, not under the command of men who had scheduled trains during most of the war and now made one another captains for yet another army they'd gladly watch march into battle. To them, I must have looked like just another conscript who needed food and a doctor. Get him that, they reasoned, and we'll get ourselves a soldier.

The next day, I marched to Padua with a handful of men more unable than unwilling to fight, mostly Slovaks and Rusyns, stripped now of the luxuries we had been given the day before and pushed into the holding pens of Austrian and Honvéd prisoners of war, most of whom looked as though they wouldn't last the night.

When I awoke in that camp, I couldn't get up off the ground on which I had been sleeping. Those of us who could walk were being rounded up and put onto trains, though no one spoke of where, and although I tried (fearing the alternative), I couldn't move into formation, I was so wracked with pain and shivering (and may even have been babbling, although all the world seemed suddenly quiet to me). An Italian guard began kicking me and shouting "*Andiamo!*" and then moved to shoulder his rifle when one of the English soldiers at the camp ordered two women orderlies to get a litter and put me in line to see a doctor.

There, the first women I had seen since Slovenia in the spring of 1917 undid the poor dressing on my hand, washed it in iodine, and wrapped it in clean linen before making a note on a piece of paper pinned to me. One was a small, oddly plump girl with a gray and pockmarked face, a local drafted into service, her white dress yellowed under the arms and soaked with blood around her chest and belly. I remember feeling self-conscious in my delirium, realizing I must smell worse to her than she did to me, and yet she took such care, all in silence.

When the doctor arrived, he spoke to himself out loud, believing, I guessed, that he was alone among a sea of triumphal victors and their beaten foes, neither one of whom spoke his language.

"These men look as though they've been living on grass and horse flesh," he said, sounding more irritated than concerned. "Not a Boche among them. What the hell kind of army is this?"

I wanted to tell him that he was right, we had been, and there was the occasional cup of tea brewed with ditch water, when we had a chance to make a fire to boil it.

All the while, he worked on my hand with distracted swiftness and telegraphed his moves by narrating them, as though consulting some other doctor in the room, though he was the only one, as far as I could tell. "Infection? Damn near. Clean shot from fairly close up. Fifth gone. Ring finger? No use. Take them both. Nurse! I'll need a tray and sutures, and change that bloody apron! No English. Christ! Okay, Fritz. Lie down. You'll never play the piano again."

After the amputation, they kept me in a bed at that poor excuse for a hospital, changed my bandages daily, and fed me. When I could stand and the risk of infection had passed, they gave me new clothes (some dead Austrian's old uniform) and shipped me out with the rest of the prisoners.

All of the trains I rode from there were old boxcars bolted shut, and I never saw daylight until we reached what a chipped and peeling sign at the station said was Livorno. And there we were boarded into the hold of an old coal-steamer ferry, which chugged across a lurching sea and landed on the island of Sardinia. The harbor town was deserted as we disembarked. Or perhaps its locals remained out of sight while this boatload of despised Austrians boarded the trains those locals rode every day from one town to another, and we disappeared in order and silence to the sentences that awaited us.

After a long journey that I reckoned was taking us south, the train stopped at a siding that could have been any stretch of track that dead-ended in a desert, or a quarry, or at the base of a mountain—anywhere that was nowhere—and we were separated by rank, marched through the gates of a compound that had been built long ago, given showers, deloused, handed clothes to wear that felt like burlap, led four men at a time into dark, bare cells with small uncovered slits cut in the stone above head height (and through which more mosquitoes came than light), and doled out a ration of a crust of bread and a tin of water. Still, it was no worse than where I'd slept at Fort Cherle and like a villa compared to the muddy pits in which we had made our stand on the Piave. I slept on the floor, not wanting to fight for a rack that served as a bed, and in the morning one of the men in our cell was dead and we were three, although we didn't announce to the guards that he was dead until after we had gotten our breakfast of more bread and watered-down goat's milk and shared his among us.

Not one of us moved on that first full day of imprisonment. The other two men had no wounds but were listless and feverish, and we all three sat or lay as though taking a short break after a long morning of hard labor and intending to get back to our work soon, but not one of us got up, not even to empty our bowels, and the place began to reek of shit. By evening, one of the prisoners was moaning quietly and the other seemed able to take shallow breaths, if he took breath at all. My hand throbbed with pain, though I welcomed it, for then I knew there was enough life in the limb for me to keep it, and my own exhaustion was simply that: exhaustion. Already I was feeling (as one of the others rolled off his rack in the dark and remained on the floor) something of the strength I once knew return to me. So I moved on to the bed and slept as well as I had slept since the night before Zlee was killed.

In the morning, both of my cell mates were dead and there was no breakfast. I was dragged out of the room past men wearing masks and dipping brooms in what smelled like buckets of lye water, and I was taken to another part of the prison and put in a cell similar to the other in everything but the window, which was of regular size but with iron bars across, and left there by myself.

MY HAND HEALED SLOWLY BUT WELL. WHEN THE ITALIAN soldier on the Piave shot me, the top half of my little finger was ripped off by the bullet, and on the march to the prisoners' sorting station, my ring finger had begun to get infected. I would surely have lost my arm, or died from sepsis, if the English doctor in Padua hadn't taken both fingers off at the palm, and I remember saying when I unwrapped my own bandages and looked down and saw my hand form the shape of a small pistol, "I won't die by the sword after all."

Daily I felt my strength increase, and I began to move more and go outside when the guards allowed it, and take in where it was they had sent me. The prison was a sand-stone compound in a valley near the town of Cagliari, to the south of the island. It baked in the heat of the Mediterranean by day and sat in the path of a cold wind funneling down it by night, and it might have been one among hundreds of prisons, for all I knew, although this one surely wasn't a temporary structure that was built to house an enemy vanquished in a war, but, rather, a prison of old merely opened to accommodate new inmates. When we were let out into the yard, all I could see were rugged mountains in the distance—they looked like they had only the night before risen fully from the earth—but I could smell from whichever direction the wind was com-ing, the faintest breath of sea. Because it was an old smell to me, and its wet, briny musk scrubbed the stench of death from my nostrils and mind (even in that prison), I began to long to smell it, the sea, and wondered how one lived so as to be near it always.

But life was still, day after day, the life of a prisoner. There is nothing more to say. Around me, men lived behind walls and died behind walls. The only difference between life here and on the battlefield was there we believed that the outcome of the war would be different, and so fought to that end. Here, we were reminded of our defeat, for although they died among comrades, death came quietly to those who couldn't hold out any longer, and into that silence, too, went all hope that we might have fought for some purpose.

Austrian or Slav, the Italians treated us with contempt, and without the English officers back on the Piave to stop them, they would have shot every last one of us, I am convinced. But the Sardinians who met our steamer (in what I later learned was the town of Olbia), herded us onto the train, rode with us on the long, slow trek by rail, marched us to our internment, and ordered our lives, were men of the hills and the mountains, who understood us and trusted us, strangely, or at least that's how it seemed to me, and so I came to love my jailers. They wanted us to live and thrive (they were visibly upset when one of us died, and so many of the men with whom I was sent there died), and gradually we ate what they ate, and those of us who stayed healthy were given coats for our outdoor work details as the hot summer months gave way to a chilly autumn, and if there was anything they forced us to do, it was to go outside.

"*Ki proiri, arreparari. . . . Ma proiri?*" they'd say in their staccato tongue (a dialect strange even to the Italian-speaking Austrian in my cell block, who came to realize what they were saying to us one day, and that they meant well). "A roof is for the rain. Do you see any rain?" And to be sure, that summer it never rained, and though we were the beaten prisoners of a lost war, the sun and sky up above were freedom enough.

Or at least enough to remember that we were there for only a short time. For, often when we returned to our cells, the thin gruel they delivered was topped with two or three olives. "*Mangia!*" they'd say, their sunburned faces stretched into a smile. And sometimes, when all I expected was water in my tin cup, they poured a half ration of their wine, scarlet and tasting of earth and drupe, as though it had come to be by the hands of some god. Then they would adopt a tone of mock authority as they dolled out this drink to me and the other men in my row.

"One word of protest from you sheep fuckers tonight and we will turn the guns on you," they'd say in the slow and measured Italian of the common soldier, a language I quickly came to understand. And guns? They had a few British Enfields that had been given to them and never fired, and some wore pistols low and loose in belts around their waists. But we were all just a bunch of sheep fuckers, they knew that, and they saw it in their hearts to have mercy on us, and I cradled my cup of wine, took in its scent as it rose, drained it, and gave in to sleep.

But not always did I sleep. Now that I was alone and flanked only by stone, the sights and sounds and smells of war were nowhere but in my memory, and yet from that more vivid and persistent life I began to see the faces of the men whom I'd held in the crosshairs of my sight before I fired on them. Their lips moved and yet they had no voice, and I knew that they thought of others who didn't know they would be the last ones on their minds, and sometimes I saw them turn toward me in surprise—sometimes terror—somehow knowing that I was watching them, and they stared back, pleading, but I took no pity. I told myself over and over that it was war, but when you do this, it is like opening a gate and then turning away, as though what comes and goes is of no matter, until you are overrun and it is too late to bar the gate again against intruders.

And so I thought of the men on the Soča, the Tolmin, and in Plava. I thought of the first man I killed, and the man who lifted his head to shout and warn the others of me. I thought of the deserters we killed, and the sergeant and the captain I hated, and any man I passed in wave after wave of shelling whose eyes seemed to say, I'm waiting. I thought of the men on lookout across our lines in Kobarid, sometimes five a day Zlee and I killed, as simply as spotting pigeons. I thought of the father and son we were roped to in the Dolomiten and the bed of ice in which they now lay, the brothers at Cherle, Lieutenant Holub, the gunners and the boy who fought and died beside me on Papadopoli Island. And I never stopped thinking of Zlee, so that when I awoke in the early morning and rose covered in the sweat of my nightmares, I sensed his presence there at the foot of my bed, as though my own will had summoned him. And I addressed his ghost and said, "Is it better where you are? Have they forgiven you for all of these?" And the ghost shook his head, and the movement of that spirit seemed to make him disappear altogether.

Soon, night after night, there was no end to the litany, as though, now that I had known war and lived, there was nowhere I could go in peace where the war wouldn't find me, and I would have gone mad were it not for the men who guarded me, who could read my face each morning and each night, and who changed my cell and my routine, and spoke to me occasionally when my food arrived, and still there was no escaping, and so I sat in my cell and prayed for death so as not to live in madness.

But on one of the days when, overnight, the wind had shifted with the seasons and the air was fresh, one of the old guards shook me awake in the morning and led me out through the yard and into a part of the prison that still held island prisoners, jailed for crimes heinous and mundane. There, they sat me next to an old man who was taking coffee in the sun, and I, too, was brought a small cup, and he began to speak of the weather and how he had been waiting for this day, when, with the wind, the entire island seemed to shift and change.

He was a Corsican and they called him "Banquo" because he had been imprisoned in the old jail for so long, he seemed a ghost himself, and no one knew what his crime had been (although he said to me, without my ever asking, that long, long ago he had killed a nobleman who had taken the virginity of his sister, and he never regretted once having thrust a knife into that man's heart and then watching him die powerless and bewildered), and this meeting became our morning ritual, so that I began to wake on my own again in anticipation of it. When I could be put back to work again, it was he who crossed the yard and accompanied me to crack stones or dig latrines and then sat in the shade and tutored me in Italian, his rough tone giving way to the patient demeanor of a schoolmaster, or read to me from Emilio Salgari's *I Misteri della Jungla Nera,* which one of the guards had given to him when he announced one day that it was his birthday.

IN NOVEMBER THE PRISON SWELLED WITH THOSE MEN OF OUR army who hadn't been killed on the Piave when the Italians crushed Austria's stand that autumn, men who were paraded into their cells, looking more like wraiths than prisoners of war, and who died without rising from their beds.

As my Italian improved, my conversations with Banquo began to become more far ranging, and he seemed to have an interest in and knowledge of life beyond those walls in a balance equal to his stoic acceptance of perpetual incarceration. On a cold day when jailers carried bodies out of the prison to a mass grave like men on a fire brigade, Banquo asked me in the yard, where we were drinking coffee and playing cards, how it felt to be alive when I saw so many of my comrades dead or dying, and I said that I had ceased to think of life or death because it seemed that I was destined to serve out the sentence of one for having delivered so well the sentence of the other, and that I saw the dead every night before I went to sleep as though they were still alive and standing before me.

He sat quietly for a long time and then said, "*Como Io.*"

To which I said, yes, like him, except that I didn't kill just one and wasn't expected to stop until I had murdered an army's worth of men.

"One or many," he said. "Still, they are dead and we are alive." If there was a difference, he said, it was that I had marched with an army and that he had acted alone, but each believed that God was on his side, for no one raises a hand without convincing himself first that he is right.

From a far-off corner of the prison, there came the sound of singing, one of the guards, for the song was in Italian and spoke of a warrior who left his home to fight for his king, and whose lover begged him not to go, but he did, and she was so brokenhearted that she took her own life, and that kingdom lost the war, and when the warrior returned home, he wanted nothing more than to be consoled in his defeat by the woman he had left for the fighting, but who was now long gone, and he grew old with his sword and his shield at his bedside.

"*Arma virumque cano,*" Banquo said, "the guard's song has reminded me of that." He asked me if I knew the line and the poem, but I said that I didn't, and he said that it was an old poem written in Latin and that he had learned it in school when he was a boy but had forgotten all of it except these first few words, and that he believed that nothing proved truer in the course of one's life than a man's incessant need to fight—even when convinced that he wants nothing more than peace—against someone, something, some other, so that he doesn't go to his grave having lived to no purpose.

"I have had enough of my purpose," I said.

"Well then, welcome to death," he said, and smiled, so that his aged teeth looked like slabs of white marble, and I did indeed feel vanquished.

That night I faced again the same parade of visitors, and when it was over, Zlee sat at my bedside, as he always did, and I said nothing this time until I awoke and the sun was already high and hot in the sky, and the guard shouted through the door, "*Russo!*" (because every Slav was a Russian). "*Tuto bene?*"

That afternoon, the sun beginning already to sink low on the horizon, the wind picking up and bringing in the fresh scent of the sea, Banquo and I sat in the lengthening shade in the yard and I told him about the faces of the men who wouldn't leave me or let me rest, the visitations I received afterward from my brother Zlee, and the feeling that it was I, more than all these others, who should have gone before them.

"Why," he said, "so that you can haunt them?" He put his hand on my shoulder and said as he stared across the prison yard, "Like the body, courage, too, is a thing weakened, especially when we are young and invincible. We can't give one the rest it needs and expect the other to protect us. Don't anger Nature with talk of wishing she had chosen differently. See to your own nature."

I told him that I had had a long time to think about the acceptance of my life and the outcome of the war, though I could not believe, after all that I'd seen, that there could be anything other than chance and misery in it.

"And then the spirits come, one by one, and when it's over, there is Zlee, sitting, not speaking, waiting, and then nodding when I can only ask if there is something wrong, until he leaves me. Except this time I didn't say a word, and he seemed saddened by this, and for me."

"Ghosts are weak," Banquo said, "and they want only to please. Don't ask him questions. His questions have all been answered. Tell him that you love him, your brother, that you are sorry not to be with him, and that this is how our fates have been ordered. Ghosts are not the dead. They are our fear of death. Tell yourself, Jozef, not to be afraid."

After a time, I asked, "What is left to be afraid of?"

And he said, "The possibility that a life itself may prove to be the most worthy struggle. Not the whole sweeping vale of tears that Rome and her priests want us to sacrifice ourselves to daily so that she lives in splendor, but one single moment in which we die so that someone else lives. That's it, and it is fearful because it cannot be seen, planned, or even known. It is simply lived. If there be purpose, it happens of a moment within us, and lasts a lifetime without us, like water opening and closing in a wake. Perhaps your brother Marian knows this."

I never saw Zlee again in that prison or anywhere

else (although there are days still when I would welcome his spirit before me, though I am fast approaching the same place where that spirit has gone). And the men, too, who haunted me began slowly in their time to fade away, so that when Banquo asked me one day if the faces of war still marched under the banner of death toward me, I said that the last time I had seen those faces, I'd addressed them and told them that I had put down my weapon and wanted to march with my back to the fight in the direction of home, and they disappeared into the morning.

"*Bene,*" he said, and, not long after, Banquo, who had saved me, fell ill with fever and never woke.

WE WERE RELEASED IN EARLY DECEMBER, THE JAILERS ONLY saying to us as they unlocked each of our cells and brought us out into the air of a frigid but brilliant dawn, "You should go now," as though it was our idea to have come there in the first place.

But there are times, even now in my life, when I wonder if I might have stayed on that island, if those Sardinian guards had given me any chance whatsoever to fall out of line on the way to that same coal steamer that had brought us across the sea, slip away, and hide forever in the house of whatever man or woman would have me. For, though I say that I longed for home, I couldn't say where that home was now. I had shed what rags were left of my uniform for a coarse shirt, trousers, and a woolen coat lined with sheepskin. I grew my first beard, thin and patchy as it was, because there were no razors to be found, and the food and work that marked my days brought some color and full-ness back to my face. I left that island looking like not an

Austrian prisoner of war but the Sardinians who had cared for me and fed me, and with familiarity came a tinge of fear at the distance and uncertainty in the world beyond that waited, so that when the steamer reached the mainland, I thought to stow away belowdecks and return for good to Sardinia, but we were under the charge of the police, and so we quickly boarded the trains that would take us to the borders of the new Italy, and an Austria bereft of its monarchy.

In Padua, we changed trains and moved northeast to Treviso, then across the Piave and Tagliamento again, rivers steely and quiet in the winter cold, but with scars of the war carved everywhere along their banks. From there, we pushed farther north to the upper valley until we came to the town of Pontebba. On the morning of the third day of our journey north, they uncoupled the car we had been riding in and shunted it off to a siding. A cold wind blew down from the Alps and I could tell that it was going to get colder, but after the close and filthy quarters of the train, the cloudless sky and sharp air were a welcome relief.

The scent of bread wafted from a bakery near the train station. Men who had thrown away or never worn a uniform walked through the streets on their way to work or a café, and women who might once have tended the wounded and who now tended goats opened shutters of shops and homes to let the winter light in. I moved slowly, more out of cautious hesitation than fatigue. I wasn't strong, but I was healthy enough. The Italian police said that the new border was just a few miles from there and that the town of Villach was directly northeast.

"Illegal immigrants will be shot," they warned. "Now go." And that was it. We set off walking, first as a

mob, then as large groups, then clusters still clinging to
some sense of security in numbers. In Austria, on the
banks of the Drava, I broke away from ten other men
who said they were going to cross into Bohemia at
Gmünd, where the legionnaires had headquarters. I turned
and followed that river east until I came to the outskirts
of Klagenfurt and the tiny village of Abtei, then turned
south into the Karawanken Range so as to avoid all gath-
erings of men. For, even with the beard, there was no mistaking me for a twenty-year-old—soldier or no—and
because these new armies of legionnaires were made up
mostly of deserters, there was a feeling in Austria and
Hungary that the war had been lost because of the Slavs.
Moreover, with no money, the countryside was the only
place I stood any chance to get food, whether by begging, stealing, or killing it, though I had no weapon with
which to do so, and yet I found myself at peace in the
mountains, feeling again that there I would not want for
anything, nor would I be put upon to serve some malev-
olent master.

I TRAVELED EAST—IN THE BROAD DIRECTION OF THE HOME I
had once known, like some migratory bird following the
compass of instinct—and came out of the mountains and
hugged the forested roads that connected the small hamlets
and villages that had once made up the lands of old
Hungary. For weeks I trekked, and in late morning on a
day when I had already been walking for several hours, I
could see from one of those roads a run-down hut nestled
deep in a hollow. Some kind of camp, I thought, or just a
poor lodging left to crumble, yet from a distance I could see
a hole in the roof and a bird's nest in the eve. It hadn't

been occupied for some time, but I thought there still might be something to eat, or something of value, inside.

As I got closer, I could hear voices, men's voices, laughing and cajoling, as if they were at a game, and speaking Hungarian, although it sounded drunken. I crept up to a front window and peered inside. There were two Honvéd soldiers, looking as though they had gone through worse than I, one sitting at a wooden table, legs crossed, drinking from a bottle, the other bare-assed and having his way with some desperate whore lying inert on the dirt floor.

I didn't want this kind of trouble, but just as I ducked down to creep away, I heard the one at the table shout too loudly for the small space, "Give me a turn! Then I'm gonna gut the bitch."

The other rolled off and slapped the girl in the face as he did so, and I could see plainly that she was just a girl. A Gypsy, it appeared, from her features, thirteen, fourteen maybe, at the most, and I could see that she was pregnant, and far along, by the looks of it. The man swaggered as he got up from the table, and she didn't try to run or roll over or do anything. I thought she might be dead until I saw her hands reach down and touch her belly, big as a globe.

"That's right, that's right," the man spit out as he pulled down his trousers. "Three Gypsies in one day, Emil, hey?" And his friend smiled with his teeth, sat down at the same table, and finished off whatever liquid swirled in that bottle.

They must have been drunk when they got there, because there was a carbine at the back of the hut, just out of arm's reach of the girl, and another one propped against the wall next to the door. They wouldn't have been so careless otherwise, or maybe they would have.

From where I crouched, I was almost within arm's reach of the closest weapon. Even if it wasn't loaded, I figured, I could use the butt of it on the bastard sitting in the chair. I crept from the window to the door, pushed it open, grabbed the rifle, and quickly checked the bolt. One round left. The man at the table was rising, his eyes wide and teeth snarling. He looked bigger, and I suddenly wondered what it was I was trying to do. He came at me fast, too fast for that room, and I shot him point-blank in the neck, and he jerked back like he was on a rope and blood poured out of him in a flume, covering my head and face, so that I was blinded for a moment. That was when the other one jumped on me with his knife, the same kind of dagger we'd all carried in the trenches. I reached up as he was about to sink it into my chest and held his hand above my head with both arms. He was strong and I . . . I wasn't so much anymore. Slowly, slowly he brought the knife toward me, as if I was losing at a game of arm wrestling, though this game wasn't for a drink of brandy. With one last gasp, I pushed his hand up as hard as I could and his whole body tensed, eyes squinting with pain and surprise, then he dropped the knife and crumpled on top of me.

The girl was standing over him, her hands bloodied, a knife in the dead man's side, right below the rib cage and into the kidney. I got on my feet and said to her in Hungarian, "You're safe now."

She kicked the dead Honvéd and spat. "*Gadjo.*"

That's what he was, just as I was. *Gadjo.* A non-Rom, no better than these same deserters who had raped and tried to kill her and her unborn baby, and as I wiped blood off my face and hands and cursed that it had fouled my coat, the girl ripped through the pockets of the soldiers and threw a mixture of gold coins and large silver buttons into the fold of her dress. It seemed like a great deal of money and trinkets for a couple of drunken Honvéd to have on them. When she was done, she stood holding her dress and the knife and looked at me as though measuring me with her eyes, trying to decide if she might not have been better off with the drunks.

"I need you to help me bury my husband," she said.

We walked out of the hut and toward the edge of the forest. There, by a tree, lay the body of man who had already been dead for a few days, facedown in the dirt, hands tied with cheap hemp behind his back while flies buzzed the muss of hair and blood and brains caked around his head. He had begun to smell like the rotting dead, a smell I had only gotten out of my nose after breathing sea air in Sardinia. The girl grabbed him by the back of the neck, lifted him, and laid him down again so that he faced upward, what was left of his face anyway.

She bent over him, began to straighten his clothes, and cried "Oh Bexhet, my poor Bexhet," and then she stopped and looked up at me. "Something to dig with," she said.

I went back to the house to get the knife and a wooden bucket I had seen near the door. When I returned, she was whispering into the dead man's ears and putting the silver buttons she had taken from the Honvéd into his pockets. "They were . . . my husband's," she said out loud. "He kept them on his jacket." And I could see, then, torn threads on the man's breast.

"What about the gold?" I asked.

"What about it? It's mine. My wedding gift. Just another *Cigánka*, you think, eh, you bastard? Shut up and dig." She used the Slovak word for Gypsy, so I knew that she had probably come from somewhere in the east and might be moving east as well, although I wanted no traveling companion and hoped to be rid of her after we had buried her husband and I knew she was able to look after herself.

It took a few hours, but we eventually made a pit large enough to roll a corpse into. We packed down the earth hard over it, then piled a pyramid of rocks, four deep, to keep the animals out until that body was nothing more than bones. It was dark when we were finished.

"We'll need to rest," I said.

"We?" she said, derisively for a young girl. "You rest. I'm going."

But she didn't move from the spot. I went back into the hut and dragged the bodies of the soldiers outside, heavy as they were. I couldn't move them far and only hoped that they wouldn't attract animals at night. There was a fire pit on the other side of the hut, and so I used a piece of flint one of the prison guards had given me before I left and the Honvéd's trench dagger (which I kept) to make a fire with a bit of burlap I found and a piece of paper the girl had discarded when she went through the soldiers' pockets. It was going to be a cold night, and for as strong as that girl was trying to be, I knew she was, at that point, little stronger than I.

I FELL ASLEEP ON THE GROUND BY THE FIRE AND IN THE MORNING ached with cold, fatigue, and hunger. I thought that the girl had left me until I heard her rustling around inside the hut, where she had gone to sleep. She came outside holding both carbines and said, "If we don't find food and somewhere else to sleep, we'll die."

She had cleaned up somehow—not a trace of dirt or any struggle she had been through from the day before. I stood up and stomped my feet to get some blood running through them, and she handed me the rifle that was loaded (I checked) and started walking, without any other word spoken.

I had seen and lived near Roma my entire life, and I knew only that they were despised and mistrusted for their singular desire to remain detached from all but their own insular culture and society. From this truth rose all other myths about them. Yet this young woman seemed not to hold in any way to that measure of mistrust around which I had been raised, and I looked upon her as she walked ahead as an altogether unknown and unsettling thing, unsettling to me on that morning (I knew then and will confess now) for her beauty. She had sloe-colored almond eyes and sharp cheeks centered by a kind of prizefighters's nose, which was broad but perfectly symmetrical and almost elegant as it drew up and out of those cheeks. Her mouth and lips were more than full—they were too large and took up the entire lower portion of her face, while somehow still looking delicate whenever she spoke, and I never saw her smile. And all of her features were framed by black hair of a hue that seemed not to reflect light so much as exude it and which she kept pulled back to each side in braids in the manner of a schoolgirl, reminding me, in fact, that she was yet a girl. A girl who had a presence and allure to her that tugged at me in a way that I had never felt in a woman or a girl in my life. When I thought of it as we walked (she a good stretch out front but never out of sight), I told myself that it was strength. Her strength was what had attracted and held me. She seemed to have a strength that I, in all of my training and soldiering, could only grasp at. And she looked down on me. I was the filthy one. I was the man whose life she had saved, "for no good reason," she'd said the first night we camped in a stand of firs and cooked the meat of a squirrel I had shot to bits. She moved about me as though I were a leper, insisted that she clean the meat herself, and doled out what portions there were unevenly, right in front of me, as though I were a child she'd just as soon backhand if I challenged her.

There wasn't much discussion, though, about anything in those first few days we traveled together—or rather, moved in close proximity to each other. The only authority I had was with the rifle, and I said to her that we should save what bullets we had left for larger game, for I could see that we were never far from a deer or two. But there was no chance of tracking and shooting one as we walked forest paths and down empty roads while she kicked stones and picked up sticks, sang to herself, or lagged so far behind that when she wanted to scold me for any number of reasons she could think of, she had to yell ahead, until I told her that she should go on without me if she had no interest in food, because I was going to sit and wait and find some game to kill. She began to cry and said that she was very hungry and was only trying to take her mind off of that hunger. And so I told her that if she could keep a fire going, I could shoot and dress a deer, and then we'd have our fill.

We found a moss floor under snow near a creek, cleared some ground and camped there for a day and a night, and had to settle for a skinny hare for our supper, and the next morning hiked back out to the road and continued our journey, although she never kicked another stone, and sang quietly to her unborn child in a voice that was close and soothing to me, as well.

When she stopped suddenly once and I asked why, she shushed me and stood stiff and still by the roadside. Within minutes, a horse and cart appeared, the driver slowed and then sped up at the sight of us, his gaze fixed forward and his mouth in a sneer as he whipped his horse into a trot, and in his wake, we went along as before.

There were any number of places we could have stopped and rested for a few days, or longer, before moving on, although to where was never clear. Old hunting cabins, good caves, glens protected by stands of pine so thick that they worked better than walls to keep out the cold and wind. Yet the girl seemed to be in search of something, not her home village so much as a place or destination she had envisioned (or knew existed) along this path and would not cease walking until we had reached it. So we continued to camp, but never more than a full day, and in the morning she would poke me awake with a stick and say in Slovak, as though she needed to be sure that I understood it was time to leave, "*Pod'me.*"

But the snows were deep when we weren't on a traveled road, and her condition hampered our progress more and more until we were lucky to go more than a few miles in daylight, and I no longer wondered to myself why I didn't just hive off as we approached a town and make my own way to the border and then home. She had become a traveling companion by now, and although we still rarely spoke, after a while we no longer suspected each other of some impending treachery, and I felt the duty of a guide, or admirer-protector, and my thoughts turned to when—

on the bank of what creek as she bent over to drink, or in the middle of the road, miles from anywhere—she would go into labor and I would be needed.

UNLIKELY AS IT SEEMED TO ME THEN, AND SOUNDS EVEN incredible now as I narrate these events, we covered as much distance on foot through the forests and farmlands of Slovenia and Hungary as our conditions allowed in the month of January 1919, and a great distance it was. And yet, our bodies weak and getting weaker, the nourishment we found along the way meager, I never feared for our physical well-being once the lingering threats of the war seemed to have abated and we found out how (or rather, she knew how) to avoid danger in the form of persons. What began to occupy me was the unspoken question of whether we would, together, make it to the end of the road we were on, which is to say, make it to the place we wanted, each to our own, to call home.

Do you see in that what was troubling me? I didn't want to leave the side of this young woman whom the Fates had set in my path, or, to be fair, in whose path I had been set, a woman to whom my speaking would itself have been unlikely, if not forbidden or ridiculed in the world, and I struggled with a desire that seemed to have been pressed down or never allowed to emerge as it might have with a young man in another time and another place, for the young men of our time had had to turn themselves when they were yet boys to a man's desire for war. But with that war over, and wandering solely through a world as though we two were the last, or per-haps the first again, man and woman alive, it was a desire to remain at her side, even if we could not touch, and witness birth as the snows melted and the days lengthened, after having witnessed death for so long.

And so it was that, after we had been walking from the setting of one new moon to another and it seemed I would spend the rest of my life afoot, regardless of where I lived, or what it was I did, and we both (though we each refused to admit this physical weakness) were approaching exhaustion from a lack of food (the game in the mountains and among the lakes and rivers we passed not as plentiful as I had hoped and expected), we came to a clearing on the edge of a forest and stopped. Up ahead, it looked as though the terrain was about to change, for there were no longer any dense stands of firs, or peaks visible in the distance. The ground looked more like clay, the trees sparser and yet heartier for having survived, although there was nothing naked or arid about the landscape, even in late winter.

There, on the rise of a hill, set some ways back from the road and framed by a stand of birch so that it wasn't immediately visible, a farmhouse stood like a cutout in a fairy tale for children. To me, it was in a place too obvious and exposed, and for that reason I was suspicious and thought that we should go on and avoid it. Yet, she looked neither tentative nor surprised to see any of this—house or farmland—standing before her. We approached slowly and I helloed the porch in German and Hungarian but got no answer. A hen scratched about the yard until I tried to catch it and scared it into a weathered but passable barn. She told me to leave it, said, "We might get eggs from that one," and pushed open the front door without any hesitation and walked inside as though she had intended to stop here to rest for a while. I slung the carbine I had been carrying at the ready over my shoulder and followed her.

What looked like a living area was clean and uncluttered, although largely because it was emptied. A white porcelain angel stood out of place on a fieldstone mantel above the hearth and there was an old photograph on the opposite wall of a bride and groom, but there was no furniture or bookshelves or anything of value beyond the personal. The kitchen was orderly, too, in its scarcity. There were some dry goods left in a pantry, but nothing to suggest anyone was coming back soon to prepare dinner. Two back rooms had been made up and then left, and the whole place seemed not a home but some Pietist's boardinghouse that admitted only the plain and virtuous. The girl rocked a shovelful of ashes from the stove, shook out the box, ordered me to find wood so that we could get a fire going, and said that I might find something to cut with in the barn. Then she began rummaging through the pantry jars and tins for what edible things might remain there and told me before I left that if I found a bucket in the barn, I should check the well at the back of the house and see if it was fouled or still drinkable. "If it is, bring me some water before you fill the wood box."

Outside, everything I needed was where she knew I could find it. A broken-down hayrack looked like it would keep us in kindling for a while. The barn had good tools that had been left hanging on a wall (where I found a bow saw and an ax that had been sharpened not too long ago), and at the back of the house, the well still had a pail attached to strong rope and a hand crank, and it splashed down after sixteen turns and came up with cold, clear springwater in it. I took a bucketful in to her, then pulled apart the hayrack and set to splitting some logs, and it occurred to me what we had stumbled upon, what the girl had anticipated, though without expecting such complete abandonment: the house of an entire family lost to the war. Father and sons had no doubt been conscripted and sent to the front, never to return. The mother and any other women left behind must have traveled to stay with relatives, moved to the city to find work and a means to support themselves, or died—somewhere, away from here—of disease or loneliness. Now there was only the dust and loess on the floors and windowsills of the place to indicate that no one would be returning to this house in any earthly fullness of time, and so that was where we stopped and lived, for the next month, it turned out, the girl and I, before it was her time.

WE HAD NO WAY OF MEASURING THE DAYS, AND IF WE'D HAD, I'm not sure we'd have kept track anyway. I would awake from the floor in the living room, where I slept always, to find her standing over the stove in that cabin, the scent of freshly brewed wintergreen and pine-needle tea mixed with wood smoke in the air, and an egg on the fire, if the old hen had decided to give one up, or strips of venison and rabbit, of which I kept us in thin supply. I searched for the wild asparagus that grew in the woods and hills around Görz and along the Soča, and for which Zlee and I had often foraged, but the dirt was too much like clay here and there weren't the tall firs of the Slovenian forests. Still, the girl managed to find some beets in a root cellar, and where the snow was melting, there was witchgrass coming through, and these and rest sustained us.

One morning over tea, as though we had known each other our whole, short lives, I asked her if she had a name

that I might call her by and she said she did but would
never tell me. When I asked why, she said, "Because then
you'll know the truth," and so I began to call her Tajna
after that, a secret that would not be told, and she seemed
to like it and began to answer to her new name.

We slipped into patterns of work, what little we could
do, patterns prescribed to us by mores we knew without
thought or effort. She remained in the kitchen whenever I
was around, and cleaned or worked at sewing an old
blanket she had found in a cedar chest when I wasn't. I
seemed drawn more to the collecting and repairing of
what tools or discarded furniture I found in the barn
than to hunting, which I did, but which I did only for the
food we needed to sustain us, so that I found myself carrying what game I might have shot that day back to the
cabin at a brisk pace, so anxious was I to return to her.

In this way, we moved into the last month of her con-
finement, like a couple that communicates by intention
nearly as much as by word, so in tune are they to each
other and their surroundings. One of the curious things
I had found in the loft of the barn was an old wooden
cradle that had one of its rockers broken off. It had a
shallow-enough arc that I could carve a new one out of
a single board with a sharp plane that was among the
tools, and so I measured the curve and set a board in a
vise and started planing, the feel of the metal on wood
drawing me back to the barn in Pastvina, the scent of
wood shavings on my clothes and strewn about the floor,
the low of a cow if the weather meant they had to remain
inside, and the whiff of manure everywhere, and I felt
nothing but mournfulness, not out of an urge to go back
there, but a realization that I would have to face one day
all that I loved and all that I hated about the place. Or

would I? And when I looked up from my work, the girl was standing in the door, her arms folded over her enormous belly and her body leaning against the door frame. Then she smiled and said, "There's hot tea if you'll take it," and waddled like a goose back toward the house.

Another time, when I came out of the barn and saw her lumbering across the yard with a full pail of water, I rushed up and took it from her and our hands touched and she let that touch linger, though she had let go of the pail, and she thanked me and told me that she was feeling tired. I carried it into the kitchen and turned to leave, when she asked me why I hadn't left her and gone my own way, "after we had killed those soldiers," she said, as though we were brothers in arms who had fought their way out of some besieged hollow. I stopped and held the back of a chair and told her that she was about to have a baby, and this wasn't exactly the kind of countryside where one might find villagers hospitable to Gypsy women, pregnant or otherwise.

What she meant, she said, was didn't I have a home, a wife, a family that I wanted to get to, and I said no, that my mother died when I was an infant, and my brother died in the war. "I have a father," I said, "and I miss him more than I thought possible when I was with him, but I'm not sure he's even alive, or if he is, if he'll want to see me now."

Why, she asked, and I said because I had rejected him and run off to war, and couldn't return as either a victor or a hero, "or even a man brave enough to save his brother."

She sat quietly for a while and then said that she thought this was sad, and she told me that for a boy, I sounded like an old Gypsy woman who sat by a stove in her house and talked about the dead more than the living. "But even this old woman is surrounded by family," she said. "In the Sátoraljaújhely, I have more family than I can count. No one is ever alone."

I asked her why, then, she and her husband were traveling alone, and she said, "Brother. He was my older brother. He was helping me to get to Ljubljana, where I was to meet up with my lover so that we could be married."

And she told me the story of having met a young first lieutenant in the Honvéd in Miskolc when she had gone there with her mother and sisters to sell lace in the market. He was right out of cadet training, on leave, and once he caught sight of the girl, he shadowed her for the entire day and the next. Their caravan traveled down to Hatvan, and he followed, this time approaching their stall and pretending to want to buy some handkerchiefs when she was minding the goods while her mother prepared food. Young herself and giddy with the delight that a man in uniform was paying her so much close attention, she returned his glances and asked him directly if there was anything of hers that he thought was pretty and to his liking.

At the meal, her mother, who had seen and heard everything, slapped her across the face and told her to keep away from such filthy men, but this only emboldened her. Surely this prince wanted only to give her beauty the recognition it deserved, and give her the life and luxury her mother and sisters could only dream of. They are jealous, she thought, and I will not let my prince go.

It was that very evening when she noticed a soldier, a young private, lingering on the periphery of the caravan, and when she went to speak to him, he said that he had been (as she suspected) sent by the lieutenant to find out all that he could discover about her, and not to return until he knew who she was, where she was from, and where she was going. So she told the private to tell his commanding officer that she and her family were to stop in the city of Eger on their way home and visit cousins there. She could slip out at the evening meal, when she wouldn't be missed, and they could meet at the fountain in the square near the castle. She pulled a flower from her blouse, gave it to the messenger, and said, "Give this to him, and tell him that he need only to come and he will find out all there is to know about who I am, where I am from, and where I may or may not be going."

Days later, after they had strolled from the fountain, through the square, up to the castle, and onto a secluded rampart, their kisses turned to his promises of marriage, and they made love, "without even so much as his coat for a pillow, and only the night above," she said, and she never saw him again.

When she discovered that she was with child, her mother confined her to housework and cooking—most of which she did anyway—but away from everyone except the old woman who talked only of the dead. All the while, her mother kept saying that when the child was born, it would go straight to the orphanage in Miskolc.

One night, her favorite brother sneaked in to see her and she told him what had happened, and that she was convinced her prince was alive but couldn't come to her because he was at the front. A few days later, her brother returned at night and took her to the house of a fortune-teller, who said she could see the young officer clearly, could see that he was stricken with love for his princess, and that he longed in his heart to be reunited with her, if only he could survive the war. Brave men often died in battle, and this man was one of the bravest, the fortune-teller assured her. The girl was beside herself with grief, so much so that her brother began to fear for her and the child. It was then that the fortune-teller added that she could see faintly the young man walking the streets of what looked to her like the old town of Ljubljana, although she couldn't be certain. He wouldn't be there long, however, for his orders back to the front for the empire's final, victorious push were imminent. If the girl could get there before his leave was over, she would find the happiness she desired.

"I must tell you, though," the fortune-teller moaned from her trance, "the journey is an impossible one. But for love, nothing is impossible."

Keeping their escape a secret from everyone, including their mother, the girl and her brother borrowed what gold and other dowrylike possessions they could the following day, and then stole out of their village under cover of night.

"Maribor was far behind us," she said, "and I swelled with the expectation of seeing my prince again, until those soldiers caught us at dusk, when we were tired and off guard. My poor brother fought as bravely as he could, but I knew when I saw them, and smelled them, that the fortune-teller had lied."

And although we never spoke at length again about that or any other story (she never once wanting to know more about my father, or my mother, only asking me occasionally where it was I—a boy, she kept calling me—learned to do the things only women were allowed to do in her village), we were rarely out of sight of each other, unless I went into the forest to hunt, and when I returned, she would embrace me and scold me for having been gone for too long, before turning back to whatever chores occupied her. After a time, then, she would come to the barn with a pot of tea, call me to a table made from a tree stump (for the weather was breaking in that part of the world and the days were often warm and springlike), take my hand, and insist I sit and drink. And I wished in my heart that we would never have to leave.

IT WAS ABOUT THIS TIME THAT WE FOUND A HORSE GRAZING on grass one morning by the side of the house. It had a bridle with a lead tied to it but was otherwise unmarked and bare. It didn't appear hurt or lame, and the girl approached it and it shied, but she held out a slice of beet and it nickered and ate and she patted its foreleg and rubbed its neck, holding on to the bridle.

"It belongs to someone," I said, "or it would have charged out of here before we got close."

"*She* belongs to someone," the girl said. "It's a mare. And what's the harm in keeping a horse if she wants to be kept?"

"No harm," I said, "except that someone might come looking for it."

The girl pared another slice of beet and the horse ate and licked her hand, so that it was covered in red, as though dyed or bleeding, and she said, sounding like someone weighing odds or options, "Let's leave her and see what she'll do."

I filled a trough with some water and we went about our usual chores the whole day as she grazed on the new grass that was beginning to come through. The next morning, the mare was still sauntering about the grounds, and after breakfast the girl went out and led her into the barn and to a stall that must have held a jennet or a mule at one time, closed the gate behind her, and the mare lay right down on the ground to rest.

For the next few days, we fed and watered her and she came out of the barn for some exercise, which meant I walked her up and down the road, then took her back to the house and let her roam. She didn't seem to want to go anywhere else. At meals now, the girl and I talked of the horses we had known, and I told her that my father's fondness for the American general Ulysses S. Grant made me believe that in war horses were treated as well as soldiers, if not better, until I went to war and found that if a horse wasn't good for pulling, it was good for eating, and shot. And if it wasn't good for eating, it was good for nothing and was left on the roadside to rot, so that the stench of a dead horse could be smelled for miles as you approached. She shuddered when I said this and told me that the horses of the Roma were as good, and sometimes better, than the horses she had heard they rode in America.

"A horse is clean," she said "and noble." And then, as an afterthought of virtues, she added, "And it can work harder than a man."

Still, I felt in my gut that this horse wasn't meant to be a blessing to us, and two days later I came out of the woods in the late afternoon after a long day of hunting, during which I netted one hedgehog and a hare, and I saw from a distance that the front door was open but the girl wasn't about. I picked up my step and looked into the barn, but I found neither the girl nor the horse, and I ran inside the house.

It was ransacked and overturned. In the kitchen, I found cupboards emptied, the table smashed, and, by the back room, the girl lying on the floor, blood on her lip and a welt below her eye where she'd been hit. I picked her up and pushed through the curtain that separated the room she slept in from the kitchen and laid her down on the bed. She was conscious and kept whispering over and over, "Where are you? Where are you?" but she kept her eyes closed, and every now and then she would wince and hold her belly.

"What happened here?" I said, out of breath and anger rising. "Who did this?"

"The boy," she whispered, "the boy," and I thought she meant the baby inside her (for she had divined some time ago that she was to deliver a son) and told her that the boy would be just fine if she lay still and slept for a while. I went out to the well and wet a rag, brought it in and laid it across her eye, and told her again to sleep. In the kitchen, I bolted the last round I had into the carbine, noticed the other one we kept with us was gone, and went outside to follow the tracks of the horse and whoever had taken her down the road.

I moved fast, as I knew there wouldn't be much light left soon, and it didn't take long before I saw the brown hide of the mare, but no one that I could discern was leading her, and I slowed so as not to spook horse or man, and when I was within fifty yards of them, I shouted at whoever was in front to stop and turn around slow.

As he did, I kept approaching with my rifle shouldered, and I could see as he stood in the road now with his hands raised, one still holding the lead, that it was just a boy, twelve, thirteen years old at the most, and I knew what the girl had meant. The other carbine was slung over his shoulder.

"You stole our horse," I said, my cheek in the rifle's weld so that I could shoot the moment he might draw a pistol or try to run.

"Your horse?" he said, his voice high-pitched but cocky for a young boy.

"Drop the lead and I won't shoot you," I said.

"Does a week of feeding my uncle's mare grass and water make her yours?"

Which is what I would have countered with if I was staring down the barrel of a rifle and a stolen horse pawed and sulled at my side. "If it's your family's," I asked, "where are they?"

"Dead," he said, "like everyone else."

"Why'd you beat the girl?"

"She came after me with a stove lid, the bitch. What are you doing living there?"

"It's no concern of yours. Not anymore. Now drop the lead and leave the horse." He stood there, not frozen or scared, just indifferent, like we'd been talking about what price he got in town for goods that were stored elsewhere. "Drop the lead and walk on," I said again, "or I'll shoot you where you stand."

He dropped the lead and brought the carbine around fast from his shoulder, faster than I thought possible, and the two of us stood in that position, duel-like. I could have killed him in the space of a breath, but he seemed pitiful to me, and yet noble for holding hard to this last remnant of his life.

"It's not loaded," I said.

"You don't know that I've got bullets, do you?"

"I know."

He lowered the barrel and pushed the rifle around to his back, hooked his thumb around the strap in one hand and the horse's bridle in the other, and stood looking at me in the dusk.

"All right, then," he said. "Shoot a man for a horse." And he let go of both strap and bridle and stood there in the road with his arms outstretched, so that the mare thought he meant to give her some room, and she stepped into the grass to graze.

I held my rifle steady and aimed for the center of his chest, stroked the stock with my trigger finger above the guard, and breathed deeply in and out to calm myself. After a while, the boy turned and gave the horse a tug and she walked off along behind him, just as they had been doing when I came upon them, and I waited until they were out of range, ejected the last round from the magazine into the dirt, heaved the rifle into the woods, where it landed in thick moss beneath an oak, and ran at a trot back to the house and the girl.

I NURSED HER INTO THE EVENING AND NIGHT, HELD HER AND wiped her face as she came in and out of a light consciousness, and then she slept for a long stretch, so that I fell asleep, too, in the chair I kept at her bedside. She woke in the darkness of midnight, shook me awake, and said, "It's time. It's broken."

I lit a lamp and looked down at the mess of sheet and ticking on which she slept and could see what looked in the light like mingled daubs of blood. She saw it, too, and said, "No, it can be that way sometimes. I was careful to shield myself when he hit me. Wash and put the water on."

But she was still ashen and sweating, and I made her lie back down in her bed after I had stripped the soiled sheets and thrown some shirts and coats over the bare frame. For a long time, she lay resting and breathing deeply, time I took to bank the stove, get more water from the well, and fill the pot to boil.

When her labor began, I knew enough to tell that it was going to be hard. I had been around many animals giving birth, and the ones who seemed stronger, as though masking a fear, were the ones for whom birth often turned from life to death. But I had never been with a woman in labor, and I wondered if I would know what to expect, what to look and listen for.

For the first few hours of her contractions, she breathed and moaned and tried to rest, and I could comfort her only with the cool, wet rag. Then, as they came closer and intensified, she sat up and panted. "Jozef, my hand, hold my hand," and she pushed down on my hand, the bed, the ground, and cried into the night, and this went on for hours as the morning came on, and then day, and what I never expected was the long resistance that child had to being born. I knew he wasn't breech. But he was turned and so couldn't move fully into the birth canal. I coaxed her and held her and tried to massage away her pain, but it grew and grew with yet more and longer hours, it seemed, the child not coming, only screams, and in my own exhaustion I weakened and buckled and wept, because in the early spring month we lived in that pastoral, waiting for this moment, I had prayed and dreamed that this girl might be some answer to another prayer I had made in a prison cell in Sardinia, that the misery and death I had dealt and seen might somehow be turned around, might somehow be wiped clean by a life unexpected.

I noticed that the sun was setting in the west, and I thought how quickly and yet full of burden a day can begin and end, and she pulled me close to her and said that if the child lived, I had to take it back to her village, that they would want it and care for it, in spite of her.

"Promise me, promise me," she whispered, her lips

brushing my cheeks. And I said that I would, and that she would come, too, because we had a long way yet to go. But she turned her head on the pillow and said, "No. It won't be. Not me. Just go. Across the Sajó. It's close. You'll see. The baby," she said, and wailed, and I knew that if she didn't deliver soon, she and the baby both would die.

But she seemed to know this as well and, without my directing her, rose from the bed and sat on the edge so that gravity might do its best as a midwife. I placed a blanket on the floor and then held her from behind for support as she clenched her fists and stood and inhaled deeply, and the screams that came were unearthly, and the power in her back and arms was enough to bring tears to my eyes and make me wonder if she might crush my own hands as she bore down.

I saw the gush of fluids then and moved around quickly to take the child from her and keep it from strangling. The head had crowned and with each push more of the face emerged, though there was no wiping away or staunching of blood, so much blood it was, as though the child must swim through it as both test and augury, for she had torn, as I had seen sheep tear when the lamb was large or ill-positioned, and I knew later, when the bleeding wouldn't stop, that something had ruptured inside.

But in that moment of birthing, I grabbed the head, fully free, and as she pushed, I worked out the shoulder caught in her tiny girl-like pelvis, and it was a boy, stiff and blue, but he bent slowly and then kicked and wakened, determined but exhausted as he gulped his first breath of air and bellowed weakly there in the cup of my arms. I tied off the umbilicus with a strip of cloth and cut it with a pair of sewing shears and then wrapped him in a sheet and placed him in his mother's arms.

She lay back on the bed. She was white and breathing shallowly, but she pulled her son to her and spoke to him softly in Romany, secrets I knew nothing of and would never hear whispered again. His bellows became mews as he searched her out in his hunger and then latched and sucked, and the two rested there.

When I returned with more rags and sawdust, she was coming in and out of sleep and looking ghostly from blood loss, but the boy clung to her and what life there was in the first and last precious drops of foremilk she fed him, until she was dead. I lifted him from her and he wailed out of longing, as I did, too, out of a grief I'd never known, so that the two of us were like a chorus of orphans lost and broken in the world. And as we sobbed, I bundled the child and made a sling on my chest out of webbing I had cut from the dead soldiers' backpacks a long two months ago, and I felt her in that house, helping me and hurrying me, as though the valley wind itself whispered, *Cross the Sajó!* I had no idea how far, or how long, I or the child would be able to endure. We were both empty of what it was we desired. I went to her on the bed, pulled the quilt up to her chin, whispered, "*Milujem t'a,*" and kissed her cheek, which was cold and pale.

In the kitchen, I spilled the oil lamp across the table and onto the wooden floor, drew a burning log from the stove and set fire to the house, ran out into the night, moonlit for the first in a long time, and began to move quickly east.

I RAN LIKE A FUGITIVE IN THE DARK, NOT KNOWING WHERE I was going, only why, and I would have run throughout the night, the next day, and another night, for all nights if

I had to, until I collapsed, because for the first time in years, since the war, since I'd embraced my father and said good-bye, I held hard to life, a life that needed me to move on this road, in this direction, waiting to come to the river she called the Sajó, if her son was to survive.

For the first few hours, he slept, squirming occasionally and crying out in whatever confusion he was capable of feeling, but otherwise he breathed in silence, lulled by the steady trot I had fallen into. I never knew exactly how far into Hungarian territory the girl and I had walked. It was she who had set the stiff pace that I'd had to condition myself to follow, so unconditioned to days of continuous walking was I after six months in prison. And not every farmer with a horse and cart passed us by without regard. One stranger or another would stop for us if he felt moved more to charity for the young girl with child than derision for her race, and we would climb onto the back of the cart and bounce along in discomfort until he indicated that he had taken us as far as he was able, and we would climb off and keep walking. She otherwise had tried to avoid all cities and towns, only rarely venturing into a local village when she recognized it as a place not inhospitable. There she'd buy a loaf of bread, cheese, or soft old apples with what few coins she had left, and then take the low road, a lift of her head the only sign to tell me that her errands were done and she was going.

So I wasn't completely certain that if I kept moving east I would come to any river in a day's time. The boy would not live if we weren't any closer, and I spoke this out loud to her as I slipped through a small candlelit village in the dark and began to doubt that I could physically do what it was she had asked of me, and said so, as though she ran beside me. But then I realized why she had stopped that day as we came out of the forest, how it was she'd seemed to know that house, and why she hadn't gone home to have her baby, even when she'd remained perhaps only a day's ride from her own family. She'd feared they wouldn't have her, wouldn't take her back and welcome her son, but would shun her, leaving her to face the world alone, an impossible thought, and so she'd hovered between remaining lost in their memory and found in their lives, and died there. And all of this conjuring made me long for her, made me wish that by some reversal of time, or miracle of divine Providence, I might return to that homestead and find her alive, and once again live and move in her presence and shadow.

BY FIRST LIGHT, I RECOGNIZED TERRAIN SIMILAR TO THAT of Kassa. Wild grapevines grew along the brown plains, and I couldn't go a few kilometers without passing some peasant setting out for a field, often with a dog that was more than willing to snap at me, so that I picked up a staff along the way and began bringing it down on the heads of at least two curs before the sun was up. The days had gotten warmer, too, so I knew that I was in the basin lands that stretched between the Duna and the Hernád. I have to cross a river soon, I thought, or a border.

I was reduced to a slow crawl by the time I saw the military truck approaching. To them, from a distance, I was probably just another villager with a pack slung back to front, and not worth bothering, but I couldn't take that chance. I ducked off the road and made for a shack where a rusted tractor, useless and idle, was parked in its permanent shade. I crouched down against the wall as the truck passed, but when I tried to get up, my legs crumbled and

I slumped over, unable to go any farther. The boy woke and began to cry, but his bleats now sounded as weak and expiring as he was. Neither one of us had taken food in the hours of which I had lost track. How much longer can he go? I wondered, and whispered to his covered head that we would be home soon, then leaned back against the shed wall to keep from smothering him and told myself I would rest there for just a few minutes, while those weakening moans haunted the air about me.

I woke, to find an old man prodding me with my staff. His body stood in the full light of the sun, which had come around to the side of the shack I'd been sleeping against. When I stirred, he bent down and pulled off the cover of the sling to see the child, and then he waved to a woman in a horse-drawn dray, helped me to my feet, and said in Hungarian (although I saw his face and knew that he was a Rom), "Quickly, the soldiers are returning."

He walked me out to the road, took the baby, and handed him to the woman, who put him to her breast. Then he waved me under a tarp that covered a load of manure piled high on the back of the heavy cart. "Keep quiet and don't move," he said, "and they'll think you're just another mound." He dropped the tarp, so that I lay curled up in darkness, and climbed aboard and nudged the horse gently on so as not to draw attention. I could hear the woman singing to the baby, felt her rocking him as we rode, and I knew when I heard her begin to cry that she, too, feared for his life.

The truck came up fast; I could tell this when I heard it brake hard in front of us and order the man to pull over. The soldiers had gotten word of an army deserter in the area, they said, a thin, bearded man carrying a walking stick and a field pack.

"Have you seen him?" they asked.

The man said that he hadn't, that he and his wife were only taking this load of manure to their village across the Sajó, and I could hear the rest of the men joke about which was worse, the stink of a Gypsy or the stink of cow shit, then footsteps crunching along the dirt and stone, getting louder as they approached the back of the dray, and then a rifle barrel poked under the tarp to lift it.

"Let's go, Ábel!" the other men in the truck yelled. "These two stink!" And the tarp lowered again and the truck drove off, shifting hard through its gears, until there was silence all around me and I wondered if the man seated in the cart and holding the horse's reins was still there with the woman and child.

I fell asleep in that bed of shit, though I was brought to the edge of waking occasionally by the ruts and rocks in the road that my driver failed to miss, until he came to a stop and threw off my cover. The noonday sun was bright and warm and I rubbed my eyes against it and looked out. We had crossed a bridge, the water below wide and brown and shallow. Along the banks to the east sat a Romany village where smoke rose from the makeshift chimneys of makeshift huts, and I watched the figures of small children emerge from one of these huts to chase a mangy dog through the dirt and mud and then disappear, although it was hard to say where. The old man told me in Hungarian that this was as far as he was going.

"Where's the boy?" I asked him, and he pointed to his wife, or daughter, or whoever she was. She flinched and pulled the baby to her. "He needs nursing," I said.

"He's being nursed," the old man said.

The woman yelled back with scorn and a heavy accent that he might have died, but the man glared at her.

I said that I was grateful for their rescue but that I had to take the boy to his home, where he belonged. "His mother was from a village across the Sajó," I said, "and I made her a promise. Give him to me."

"This is the Sajó," the old man said, and pointed to the water with a long sweep of his hand. "Who is this woman you're speaking of?" he asked, and I couldn't answer. I never suspected that the truths and lies she had gathered and spun for her tale of love and wandering would mean nothing without a name she had refused to give, or even without thinking might have spoken. "I don't know," I said. "I don't know her name."

"I see," he said, disbelieving my own story of deliverance. "The boy is being nursed, and he looks strong enough to survive. You've done what your . . . lover asked you to do, no? He'll be safe with us."

I reached for the dagger I kept in my boot and held it up weakly to the old man. "He comes with me," I said, but the man stood there unfazed. The woman uttered some incomprehensible taunt or invective and he nodded his head but otherwise said nothing more and didn't move, and I realized then that I had made a stand with the intent to kill not for the baby, whose eyes I can say I had never seen in the light of day, but for a promise to a woman who would have considered my love a taboo, and whose ashes lay beneath the smoking rubble of a house in the forest, ashes that one day soon would be lifted by the wind, and my knowledge of this would be more than any one on earth could say they knew of her.

By this time, the villagers had begun to wonder why we three stood unmoving near their bridge, and people started swarming up the banks for a closer look, shocked to see one of their own being threatened with a knife. Some shouted their own threats, and a boy who could not have been more than ten kept saying over and over in a Hungarian he'd probably learned in school, "Fight me! Fight me!"

Then the man, some kind of elder—this was clear to me from the response of the others—held his hand up to the crowd, commanded their silence, and asked me in a quiet voice, "The boy's mother, was she a young girl?"

I said she was, and that she'd been traveling with her brother. "When I came upon them, he had already been killed by Honvéd. Deserters, I'm sure they were."

"And where are these deserters now?" he asked.

I told him that I'd killed them when I saw what they were doing to the girl, and he feigned surprise at this. "You killed a Hungarian soldier in order to save the life of a Gypsy?"

I told him that I'd killed one soldier and the girl had killed the other in order to save my life, but that I had killed many men in the war without regard for what coat they wore or what language they spoke. It was all the same to me.

"Did you kill her brother, too?" he asked.

"No. I told you," I said, "he was dead already. I helped her to bury him."

"That seems unlikely," he said, "since we have our own rituals for burial." Someone else shouted from the crowd that I should be turned over to the police so that they wouldn't think the villagers were harboring deserters and return to arrest them and burn their houses.

I told them that I wasn't a deserter, that I'd been a prisoner of the Italians, and when the war ended, they'd released me, put me on a train to the border, and left me to walk home.

"You've come a long way, then," the old man said, and the crowd went silent again, as though wondering who would move or admit to defeat first, I or the old man. What could I say to convince them, though? And I wondered in my exhaustion if it was even worth it. If I started walking now and followed the road in front of me to wherever it might lead, I would have done all that I had promised I'd do, even if it meant that I'd likely be inside of a Hungarian prison by nightfall.

"What's your name?" he asked, and I told him. The boy began to bawl from underneath a covering shawl on the woman still sitting in her seat atop the dray, and it sounded to me like the strongest cry I had heard him utter yet in his brief life. What does it matter, I thought, if this village or some other raises him? What will he know of life, his mother, or even me, regardless? He will grow, learn, love, fight, and die, and someone, whether he knew them or not, will deliver him into his grave.

And I remembered how she had wept over the body of the brother she'd called her husband, and so I said to the old man, "Bexhet. Her brother's name was Bexhet," and I sheathed the knife and turned to go.

I WALKED ACROSS THE BRIDGE AND CONTINUED DOWN THE road in the direction from where I'd come, or where at least I thought I had traveled from. The sun was high and warm, the air dry, and green shoots of whatever grains or tubers farmers and tenant farmers planted here protruded from furrows that came right to the ditch at the edge of that road. The stillness of a midday at rest in spring was a world I was content to walk through in whatever moments of stillness and freedom I might have left to me. And yet I walked in that direction with the conviction, if not the belief, that I could resurrect her still, even from ashes, and so I would go there, come what may, or who (for I would have been executed as a deserter once the police found me), because it was what I thought of as home.

It seemed as though I had been walking for days when the old man's horse and cart pulled up next to me on the road. He motioned for me to climb up and then turned back in the direction of the village, no more than a few miles away. And he told me as we rode that his son Bexhet and his daughter Aishe had left them months and months ago, after Aishe became pregnant by a Honvéd field officer. The community blamed her and her insolence for this shameful indiscretion, but within the immediate family they found themselves at fault for not reading the signs, for not believing that this *gadjo* was capable of seducing their daughter, and that she would find him anything more than a rogue.

"Perhaps," the old man said, "perhaps she did love him. And—I will say this only to you—perhaps he loved her, too."

The last they knew, a fortune-teller, whom they had since driven from their midst, convinced Aishe, and Bexhet with her, to run away to Ljubljana in search of the young lieutenant, although she confessed that she knew nothing of where the officer was and had only heard someone speak of the old city that day as a place where the emperor had kept headquarters during the war. An old woman who never slept and who was prone to seeing things as a result said she'd caught them stealing about on the night of their disappearance, but they gave her no mind.

"It turns out that was the last anyone had seen or heard of them. Until we had heard about you. No officer, it's clear," he said, his eyes still fixed to the road, "but Aishe loved to exaggerate. She was my youngest daughter."

When we returned to the village, life seemed as I might have imagined it there yesterday, untouched and unworried, no one suspecting who or what was to come. Two stern spinsters washed me and trimmed my beard (I wanted to keep it to avoid looking like a soldier), and I was invited to sit with the king of the Gypsies—the old man himself—while we ate and spoke of a promising crop of potatoes that year, if the spring weather was any indication, and the beautiful new foal that had been given to him by a distant relative for his kindness to a brother during the war. Then he raised his glass and said, "To the vine, who has brought one of our own back to us. May there be many branches."

Strangely, there was no more talk of his daughter, no request for me to tell of how she died, or what we might have spoken of in the last few months of her life. When I asked out of concern if someone could tell me how the child was doing, they laughed and said that he was fine.

"Already the women call him Bexhet and coddle him. A boy that strong will grow up to be a greater king than I," the old man said, a boast that sounded unlike the one who wouldn't believe a word I said and yet was still willing to spare my life.

In the morning, I joined a caravan of wagons that was traveling along the Hernád into the Sátoraljaújhely. I asked them before I left if I might see the boy and look into his eyes, so that I would have something to remember him by, and they brought him out into the dawn, shadowy and crepuscular, but he was awake and moving, having already nursed, and I could see his mother's hair, silky black and thick on his head, and her lines around the nose and mouth, but I knew that he would have his troubles in life, too, with the Rom, for his eyes—a blue

the likes of which I've since seen only in the same morning sky on the open ocean—had to be his father's, and I
kissed him on the forehead and wished him great peace
and purpose.

I traveled with them under cover of the band on its
way to the marketplace until nightfall, when I slipped
away to cross into what was now the nation of
Czechoslovakia. I longed only to see my father again, if
that gift might possibly be waiting for me, and I held out
hope still.

I DON'T REMEMBER SLEEPING WHEN I REACHED KASSA. I
skirted the city and its flimsy checkpoint—a guard shack
that stood on the main road, as though every other access
to this country had a wall keeping people in or out—and
kept walking north, past Eperjes and farther on up into
the mountains. It took days. I must have eaten something
and slept somewhere, but nothing of it stands out from
that long trek. Nothing. What I do remember is being
passed by a lone Gypsy with horse and cart on the road
into Pastvina, a young man bouncing along behind a small
but strong horse. He slowed as he approached and I
thought he might stop, but when I turned to greet him, he
yawed the horse and kept on.

It was morning when I came around the hill and
could see the spire of the church rising through the morning mist. The village was quiet. I crunched along through
a blanket of frost, crusty from the freezing nights that
hung on still this far north and into the mountains.
Smoke rose from huts and I could hear the sound of cocks
crowing randomly from inside the muffled interiors of
barns. All the sights and sounds of a place just as they

were before I wondered if I would ever see that place
again. Smoke was rising, too, from the house I had grown
up in—grown up in, that is, when I wasn't in the mountains. The thought of seeing my father suddenly made me
quicken, and as fast as I was able (which wasn't very
able), I ran the last hundred yards and opened the door
without even considering who or what I would find after
two years and a war.

My stepmother was inside, alone. She startled and
screamed when she saw me and dropped onto the floor
the cup of chickory she had just brewed. The porcelain
smashed into slivers and black liquid splashed both our
feet. I looked down at my boots and then back at her.

"*Bože môj!*" she cried out, and crossed herself.

I stood still and wondered if I should embrace her, but
she began to back away from me slowly until she found
the edge of the kitchen table to steady herself and sat
down. Her hair had rangy streaks of gray in it and her
face, always lined with the contempt she held for everyone except her sons, looked etched with an ugliness she
had carried inside for a lifetime and which now visibly
framed her. She dropped that face into her leathery hands
and began to cry.

Am I wrong? I thought. Has she found some peace on
this side of her own drawn-out battles and war? I sat
down across from her, took her hands into mine, and held
them, but she looked up, her eyes flaring red like a rabid
dog's I'd once watched attack a lame horse just before
someone shot it, and said, "Why aren't you dead like the
rest of them?" Then she got up and left me alone at that
table in the kitchen.

I sat there until the stove went cold. I had gotten so
used to the outdoors that I felt uncomfortable in the heat

www.saclibrary.org

Sacramento Public Library

Thank you for visiting the library!

DUE DATE   11-28-15
BARCODE   33029092629999
TITLE   The sojourn / Andrew

DUE DATE   11-28-15
BARCODE   33029067022228
TITLE   Falling in love / Donna

Item(s) Checked Out

11/05/2015

behind four walls. I thought, too, that it might be the only way to get the old lady to come back and face me. I wanted to tell her how—*how,* not *why*—it was that I was not dead like the rest of them. But when she did come back, wrapped up in a quilt she kept on her bed, it was only to drop a mildewed leather folder in front of me.

"This is all your father left you," she said. "Don't worry. There's no money in it. I checked." She cackled like a bird and walked back into her bedroom and closed the door, to die, for all I knew, or even cared.

There were papers inside the folder, one from the United States of America's Department of State, certifying the birth of Jozef Ondrej Vinich in Pueblo, Colorado, on the thirty-first of March, 1899. The signatures of my father, Ondrej Pavel Vinich, and my mother, Magdalena Rose Sabo Vinich, were scrawled beneath the typed "PARENTS," the ink as black as it must have been when they were alive and believed these marks would mean somehow a better life for all of us. Along with this was a letter from my father to me, written in English and dated the thirtieth of November, 1918. It was a thick ten pages of scrawl, and I wondered what it was he'd had to say, or if maybe he'd just been some kind of fool after all and these pages would only serve to remind me.

My Dearest Jozef, the letter began, *with winter has come the end of my shepherding, and with the end of shepherding will come, soon, the end of what I have tried to make of this life.* He was writing, he went on, from his bed, unable to get up and do any work anymore. He had sold what was left of his flock and let someone else do the business of taking care of other people's animals. My stepmother took from him all the money he had left and spent it before it was worthless with the advent of the new Czechoslovak koruna. He had hoped to live past the end of the war, to see Marian and me come home as heroes, but he feared he would die before that happened, and now that the war was over, he believed death had taken us all. *Still, I hope*, he wrote. *Hope that you are lost but alive somewhere. Or, having been wounded, perhaps, are resting in order to regain your strength before you come back to me.* He spoke of what news he heard of the war from those few men who had come back to Pastvina, but knew, too, that they could tell him and the others no more than what they had seen, and often suffered, so that everyone merely hoped and prayed and resigned themselves to the reality of Austria-Hungary's defeat.

Then he explained the papers. Although he had told me about my mother and their life in America, there was much left unsaid, much left yet to do, and he wanted most of all, before he died, to give me a better life, if life was still a gift God granted me. Enclosed was everything I needed to leave Pastvina and go to the United States. I was a citizen there and wouldn't need any visas or permits. All I had to do was present myself at the new American embassy in Prague, show them these documents, and I would be issued a passport.

How, though, you must be wondering, he went on to write, fully eight pages into the letter by now, and I was. This, he explained, was the reason for the old folder, the American papers, the news and sentimental wanderings, and the impression that he was a broken man with little to give. All had to be done so as to convince Borka that nothing my father had left me was of any value. Although he had enjoyed writing of reminiscences, as it began to make him feel as though he were speaking to me in person, the letter was long so that my stepmother wouldn't be tempted to send it off to a translator in Eperjes if she suspected my father was passing along any information about money or valuables. For, buried at the end of that letter, was this:

In the late fall of 1917, after Zlee and I had been gone for almost two years and my father knew that he was too old to go back to shepherding on his own, he walked up to the camp one last time in the winter to leave for me there the small fortune he had brought with him from America in 1901 and had kept hidden from my stepmother for seventeen years. Not silver, which is what he mined for the Canterbury Mining Company in Leadville when he and my mother first arrived out west, but gold, a good stash panned for and collected over the years before I was even born. It came to a little more than five ounces, but at the time, after the war, gold was worth over twenty dollars an ounce, and one hundred dollars would go a long way. He hid it in that same cavelike overhang of rock on Krížik Ridge that we used for shelter when we were away from the camp. At the back of the cave, there was a large loose stone with two thin veins of crystal running through it. The gold was behind that in a sheepskin sack. *If you never read this letter, or never return from the war*, he wrote, *then that gold will go back to the earth, from where it came. Or make some poor shepherd a believer in miracles one day. But if you do come back, and all of this makes it into your hands, go, my son. And may you find your peace there. S Bohom.*

My stepmother shook off her false grief and came out to stoke up the stove just as I was finishing the letter.

"He was a silly old fool in the end, your father," she hissed. "Kept moaning about how he had nothing to leave you if you made it home from the war. *If*, I told him.

And then he produced that musty old folder and said to make sure you got this so you'd at least remember him. Hah!"

I told her that I needed nothing to remember him by, and she said, "Nothing. That's what you got in the end," and looked at me to see if she might be mistaken.

But I acted as cold as if I was about to put a bullet through her head at four hundred yards and said, "I'll be expecting my meal at noon," so that she'd think I had nowhere else to go.

I waited at the house for a few days, visited my father's grave, which seemed cold and unreal to me, but I otherwise remained a recluse in the barn, where I slept. I could tell that snow was on the way, so I lingered until the front came in, packed up some food and found the shotgun in the barn, which, surprisingly, my stepmother hadn't managed to sell. Shells my father kept in a false floor were still dry, without any apparent rust around the primers, and so I armed myself, thinking the old gun just might come in handy. He had hidden the field glasses and a good hunting knife in there, too. The knife was still sharp. But there was no trace or mention anywhere of the Krag, not in the letter, not in Borka's enmity, not in the barn.

I left the next day before sunrise in the middle of a freakish and substantial spring storm, which covered my tracks almost as quickly as I made them. The climb out of Pastvina seemed easier, in spite of the deep snow. No month-long packs of provisions, no mule, no horse, but no one else, either, to accompany me. I missed my father and Zlee, and the kind of world I knew before I marched off to war, and the old terrain seemed worn to me, the hills less challenging, the vistas not vast so much as merely broad from where I stood, as though what once to the boy appeared daunting mountains had become in the sight of the man merely stones.

At the camp, I waited for the storm to taper off, but it seemed unwilling to let up, and when it blew over, two feet of fresh powder blanketed the hills. I cleared the cabin of a few rodents and one big snake cold and still under a crate that had once held potatoes. I got the stove going, made some tea, lit the old oil lamp, laid out my supper of bacon and beetroot, and sat listening to the night, wishing I could summon into my presence the ghosts of everyone who had gone before me—friend or foe, civilian or soldier, family or Gypsy—embrace them, and send them home. But I rested now as they had left me. Alone.

I had enough food for three days, and so I waited that long before I hiked up to the ridge and climbed inside of the cave, which still smelled faintly of the fires we used to make there, the wall closest to the opening blackened permanently with soot. And, there in the back, out of the light, so that it would have been easy to miss, I found the stone veined with quartz. I pried it loose and lifted the sack from its resting place.

Five ounces of gold is a heavy five ounces. It felt odd in my pocket, as though it would weigh me down and keep me there, rather than become my means of departure from a world and a place in which no one would mourn for me should I disappear without a word or trace.

I climbed up onto the ridge—the sun high and growing warm again as it melted the snow—and suddenly felt the unmistakable presence of my father and the comforting shadow of Zlee, as though I might turn and find them both climbing up behind me on this same outcropping of boulders to shout "Jozef!" and come to me and embrace me.

But there was no one, just the wind, and the rustling branches of a lone tree, and I knelt down and began to weep and then wail like a child, an infant at his birth, in my naked grief and desolation, howling for who and what I wanted most to touch and see, all of which had been taken from me, and at this I lowered my head and dug at the rock as tears streamed down my face and my fingers began to bleed, until I rolled over sobbing onto my side and fell asleep.

WHEN I CAME DOWN OFF OF THE MOUNTAIN, I TOLD MY stepmother that I was going to Pozsony (although word had just come east that the city was now called Bratislava) to join the Czecho-Slovak army and asked her for money for the train ticket. She said it was about time I decided to do something so that I could send her a regular salary, and for that reason only, she gave me the fare, which wasn't a small sum, as it's almost a full day's journey from the east to old Pozsony. I cleaned up the shotgun and sold it in Kassa, along with the field glasses and knife, and with that bought a ticket clear to Prague, where the new country's economy was booming. Prague seemed like a land from a fairy tale to me, and so I distrusted it for that reason, staying only long enough to sort papers and book a train out of there. I got a good exchange on an ounce of gold, mailed the advance my stepmother had given me back to her in a letter, saying that I had been sent to Prague for induction, then received my American passport at the new consulate and boarded a train for Hamburg, Germany.

Although I had never been so far west or north before, crossing that border into Germany was like crossing back into the misery of the war, fields untended, little food to be had anywhere for any price, and entire towns eerily empty of men. There were old men, and there were children, but anyone who might have been of fighting age and fit to do it had given his life, or any number of limbs, to that fight. Western Europe seemed to me a place wherein no one lived any better than we had for centuries in our miserable corner of the northern Carpathians.

The travel agent in Prague told me that I was to meet a boat called the *Mount Clay* in Hamburg, an old troopship converted to a passenger steamer, but that he was uncertain as to when exactly it was scheduled to arrive and embark again for the United States. I thought that I had missed it by the time I arrived, but it turned out that it was two days late, and then took two more days to disembark its passengers and resupply, due to the lack of longshoremen. Those were a lost and empty four days—bleak skies, a chill drizzle, and everyone starving, though too tired even to look for food. All I remember about that city, apart from my steamer at dock on the river, is the unlikely number of trees and the amount of unbroken ground that shaped its environs. More ships came into its port than any other place in Europe, and yet I felt as though I was spending a week in a country house on a lake, one whose inhabitants consisted entirely of mute and starving prisoners.

When we boarded, I went below to survey my tiny room in steerage, though the smell of diesel and the stale air reminded me of the train I had taken after leaving Sardinia, and so I walked back up on deck, in spite of the rain, which kept others under tarpaulins or down below. I looked across the river to a flock of derricks idle and waiting for freight either yet to come or that had never showed. A figure moved slowly among them and then stood in full view of me—a man, a dockworker perhaps, as idle as the steel that surrounded him, and yet seeming fit enough to walk, which was something. I tried to calculate the distance between him and me, but I was suddenly disoriented and lost my entire sense of direction. I put my head in my hands and rested them on the rail to steady myself. Below, the current swirled brown and in eddies along the side of the ship. When my vertigo dissipated, I looked up and glanced downriver to where the water bent and rose to the horizon until it disappeared. I turned and searched for the worker, and there he stood, still on the shipyard bulkhead. He lit a cigarette and gazed at our transport, and I had the urge suddenly to respond to his searching and to make my presence known. I raised my arm above the parapet of deck railing and waved in a gesture that was all at once greeting, salute, and leave-taking. He returned my wave as though he had come here just to see me off, flicked his cigarette into the water, and disappeared amid the forest of cranes and rigging.

THAT WAS THE END OF MY SOJOURN IN WHAT A FEW AROUND me here still call "the ol' kawntree," though it is no country for which I long or somehow miss in my old age, when memory is supposed to ease and there comes a forgiveness with forgetting. It will always be a mourning land, a place longing for redemption, for there is no end to the memory of it, no chance of forgetting, and so I knew that day that I would have to go home, though I wondered what would await me there in the country in which I was born but had never belonged. If I would be welcomed after my time away. If I might begin again in a manner befitting one who is no longer a soldier or even a son, just a man, with so much lost behind me, and so much left yet to be done.

The gangplank backed away, and the *Mount Clay* gave one prolonged blast from her pilothouse. Smoke-stacks puffed black diesel fumes that hung low and heavy on the harbor in the rain, and we seemed the last to leave a place decimated by plague. The ship slipped her lines and a tug nudged her into midriver, where she stalled briefly, waiting to see that everything that lay before her on the course below was clear. Then Hamburg, and Europe, and all her empires, all I had ever known—the only ground that up until then had fed me, the only well from which I had drunk—receded in slow swaths of wash and sky as we surrendered to the outgoing tide on the Elbe.

ACKNOWLEDGMENTS

The author wishes to thank the following for their generous help in the writing of this story: Lt. Col. Guy Bartle-Jones, Warren Cook, Paul Cornish (firearms curator, Imperial War Museum, London), Jared Crawford, Royal Hansen, Faith Johnson, Matthew Meyer, Renata Meyer, Gianluigi Panozzo, Virág Sárdí, Michael Silitch, and Claudio Siniscalco. Special thanks to Erika Goldman, Betsy Lerner, and as always, Amelia Dunlop, for her unwavering support.

Also, a debt of gratitude is due to the following writers and their work: George H. Cassar, *The Forgotten Front: The British Campaign in Italy 1917–1918*; Isabel Fonseca, *Bury Me Standing: The Gypsies and Their Journey*; Martin Pegler, *Out of Nowhere: A History of the Military Sniper*; John R. Schindler, *Isonzo: The Forgotten Sacrifice of the Great War*; Peter R. Senich, *The German Sniper 1914–1945*; and Jan F. Triska, *The Great War's Forgotten Front*.